I0520093

DECEPTION LICENSE

Author
R.J.Red

Editorial Consultant
Halim Altinisik

Publisher
Cosmo Publishing

ISBN 978-1-949872-14-9

"The color of truth is gray."

Andre Gide

CHAPTER ONE
COMING TO AN END

Washington, D.C.

It was just another day for Oleg. As usual, he was checking if the cargoes had been distributed to right regions by the personnel. In the meantime, he was taking a glance at his co-worker Jessy's generously exposed legs.

Noticing Oleg's glance at her legs, Jessy quickly covered and closed her legs. Oleg was busted big time. But it seemed Jessy wanted him to see her legs up to her crotch and preferred to wear a long-slit skirt. It seemed like she was making a pass at him.

He was just about to invite to her out for a drink tonight, but he suddenly noticed something outside. He saw that Vasili, the contact officer of Russian Foreign Intelligence Service (SVR - Slujba Vneshnei Razvedki), was leaving restaurant banners on cars parked on the street where Oleg's office is.

The banner with green background meant that Oleg and his wife, Viktorya, should immediately go to the restaurant. However, it was still early. He had to wait till his lunch break to go to the restaurant. It would cause suspicion if he goes to a restaurant at 9:35 am where they don't serve breakfast.

Oleg and Viktorya had been role-playing as a married couple for some time. He called home to say that they will go out for lunch and that he will pick her up.

After picking up Viktorya, they went to the Italian restaurant run by Ivan. As soon as they sat at the table, they ordered their meal. Oleg was excited, but he did not want Viktorya to feel it. It was the mission they had been waiting for the last six years. He just wanted to eat Gennaro pizza for two and leave. But the rules did not allow it. So, they ate their pizza slowly and shared the cake they've ordered.

He asked for the bill. He took the receipt from the bill box brought by Vasili and engraved the 9-digit tax number on the receipt in his memory. It was the cipher of the address they will go to.

Oleg quickly deciphered it and memorized the address. He put the money in bill box. He told Viktorya that he needed to go to restroom and would be back soon. Viktorya mocked him, "Whenever you drink beer, you run to toilet." They laughed.

Oleg tore the receipt before he went in, sat on the toilet seat, pitched the receipt into the toilet between his legs, and flushed the toilet before standing up. Oleg congratulated himself. Nobody, not even Viktorya, has seen the paper. The waiter brought the change, they tipped and thanked him before leaving the restaurant.

The first number was three. This meant audio surveillance. The second number was seven, which was the code of a district. And the next couple of numbers were codes of streets and alleys in that region. The last digits indicated numbers of the building and flat. The time on the receipt was the current time, which meant that they should immediately go to the address and wait there.

Oleg got into the car and took the regular map printed by the courier company. The numbers on their ciphered map were either one bigger or smaller than the numbers on the regular map. So, he quickly browsed through the map, found the district, street, and alley they needed to go to.

Viktorya was silently watching Oleg, and she couldn't stand it anymore. "What is the first number?"

"Three," Oleg said.

Business was going on as usual at the branch office of the courier company. Everybody was minding their own business. Oleg was the branch manager. No one would ask him why he was late, so he set off with the company car. There was nothing extraordinary when they arrived at the address, and Viktorya walked to the street door to determine where to locate the laser microphone. The street door was closed. Their target was flat number five. To make sure he would ring the right doorbell, he decided to ring all doorbells from top to bottom. He rang the first doorbell, but there was no answer. He rang the second one.

When someone answered him through intercom, he said he needed to deliver an international package to the flat downstairs but there was no one home, so he wanted to put a sticky note on the door. The door opened. He said thanks and went inside.

In order not to draw attention, he took the lift to the second floor from the top. There were two flats on each floor. He tried to hear the voices coming from the flats as he went down the stairs.

He went out and got in the car. They drove up at the end of the alley, stopped the car, and began waiting at a distance from where they can see the building. There was no action. He pointed out the flat's location to Viktorya. They should be listening to the right flat. People in the cars passing by could not see inside of their car because the windows were covered with film.

They had a laser microphone inside a small courier box, which made things easier. Then, Viktorya pointed the lens of a pinhole camera inside another small courier bag at the building.

A car passed by and stopped ahead of them. A tall and strongly built man got out of the car. The man calmly and slowly walked to the building, opened the door with a key, and went in. Viktorya zoomed in on the man.

About ten minutes later, a second car appeared and stopped in front of the next building. After a while, the right door of the car opened, and a 1.60-1.65 tall buxom woman got out of the car and smoothed down her skirt. Then, the car drove off. Viktorya zoomed in on the woman's face and the car's brand and plate number.

She could not open the street door with her key. She tried another key, and this time the door opened, and she went in.

Thanks to the microphone they had placed earlier, they heard that the people who went in were talking about a certain district without mentioning its name and without addressing each other by name. It was obvious that they were looking at a map.

They were heavily engaged in listening to them, and when they heard a knock on the window, they startled. There was a woman holding her dog's leash. Viktorya turned the safety lock of her 7.65 Baretta in the inside pocket of her jacket and rolled down the window.

"I live in number 36 at the end of the road. Is there a delivery for us from Canada?" asked the woman.

"No," Viktorya said and rolled up the window.

Viktorya and Oleg thought that they are demasked. But it was impossible. It just might be a coincidence. It was impossible to see inside the car, and besides, the car was not running, so their parking lights were off.

They were still trying to find out if it was really a coincidence—was the woman just walking her dog and stopped when she saw their car? —but a bullet crashed the rear window and struck Viktorya's throat. A second one hit Oleg in the head. Their heads hung down, and they died at the scene.

Two Days Later

The secret service investigated Viktorya's and Oleg's deaths, but their unit was willing to make their own investigation. They sent a cipher message to Aleksandr, another sleeper agent like Viktorya and Oleg, via a computer game and commissioned him to investigate the incident.

As soon as he received the message, Aleksandr left the building to go to the crime scene he saw on television.

He cautiously looked around when he was out and walked around his car as if he was checking the tires. But just then, a remote-controlled bomb placed under his car exploded. He died on the spot.

*

Moscow

While Russian intelligence analysts were trying to understand what happened, news sites on the net published that the victims were from SVR.

Headlines of newspapers were interesting. One said, "horrific execution." The public was asserting that the aim of the incident was to discredit Russia. Countries opposing Russia and nongovernmental organizations were commenting that the incident was a major blow for Russia.

Nongovernmental organizations held protests in Washington D.C. to condemn the incident, Russian agents in their country, and those who did the killings.

In the meantime, SVR headquarters remained silent and everybody was feeling down. They knew that if the American government detects their sleeper agents, it would follow them closely to find out their activities. Nevertheless, they couldn't make sense of why their sleeper agents were killed. Why did they kill them instead of catching them on the act and forcing them to change sides?

White House spokesperson made a statement and declared that the US has nothing to do with these assassinations and the suggestion was a provocation aimed at damaging the relationship between America and Russia.

At the meeting held in Kremlin, it was decided that their sleeper agents should not be discovered, so the embassy pursued the standard procedure and denied having any part in the incident. The official statement made it clear that the said persons were not connected to SVR or any other intelligence agency and condemned the US for not protecting their citizens' lives.

Later in the day, arguments regarding the existence of a mole caused disturbance at the meeting of the Russian Security Council, and the SVR director had a very hard time.

"In the right place and at the right time, a spy is equal to thousands of soldiers at the front. Believe me! When you look at the results of a war, bravery of artillery, cavalry and infantry will be pale in comparison to this damned invisible army of spies!"

Napoléon Bonaparte

CHAPTER TWO
THE BEGINNING OF THE END

Galina lived her childhood and youth in a family where her bad-tempered and alcoholic father always beat, mauled, and swore at her mother for no reason.

Galina's mother, Darya, had suffered a great deal of traumas. The last one was in 1991, just before the collapse of the Soviet Union, when the Soviet government has expropriated all bank accounts due to economic downturn.

It was normal for an economy to be disrupted where everyone was working for the state but not actually working.

After the dissolution of the Soviet Union, or according to some, conscious fading of the Soviet Union from the stage of history, the wreckage of the Soviets gave birth to unemployment, social crises, suicides, gangs, seizure, rape, alcohol addiction, and divorce. Inflation reached 2,500%, and people's savings were reduced and even melted away. Those with money had already left the country, and those who couldn't were making plans to leave soon.

It was difficult to find happy people in Russia then. Everyone was quick tempered, and even the smallest things led to quarrel and fight. Only the Soviet elite and drunkards were happy. Those who sought to solve their problems with alcohol were fooling themselves into thinking they had no problems, and they had a good life if they kept drinking. When they became sober, they are faced with reality and become unhappy again. While they were fooling themselves by messing around the drunkard-sober dilemma, the Soviet elite was busy with seizing state properties and selling the weaponry of the Red Army.

Social structure was so degraded, and many cops were not going to crime scenes for reported crimes like burglary, seizure, and kidnapping; they took no notice of anything.

Like all Russian youth, Galina aspired to live like Europeans as she watched European lifestyle on television. She was especially not missing Peter Esterman's shows and beauty contests.

Darya's last trauma was of losing her job in the yarn factory when factories were shut down one after another. Actually, she knew she was going to lose her job months ago. Because the factory could not pay their wages. In order to earn money, she was working at night clubs till 5:00 am and at restaurants as a cleaner, receiving her daily wage as soon as she finished her work.

She was trying very hard not to paint a pessimistic picture as she didn't want Galina to be affected by these problems. Whenever they talked, she kept saying, "My sun! These hard times will come to an end! Please don't worry!"

When the factory was shut down, she became a casual worker at a tailor shop. She was not a cleaner anymore.

Whenever Galina asked her mother why she didn't leave her father, who was 21 years older than she was, Darya couldn't give a real answer; Galina insisted she was brushing her off by saying, "Could it be because I love him?"

There always had been an invisible wall between Galina and her father. He never bounced her on his knee or played with her. Galina had thought for years that her mother had tricked her father and gotten pregnant on purpose. Her father was indifferent to her mother. He was a very different person in front of others, a positive man. He always made a pass at their beautiful neighbors in the apartment, and when he got drunk, he read poems to his friends.

Galina decided to be psychiatrist when she was a middle school student just to convince her mother to divorce her father. But the bribe her mother gave was only enough for her to enroll in the Department of Turkish Language and Literature.

Galina met Maksim the day she went to enroll in the university. Maksim fell in love with Galina at first sight.

On the first day of class, Maksim wore his best clothes and went to the university very early. He looked for Galina everywhere. His heart was in his mouth and couldn't sleep that night.

Russian universities strangely had gym classes. But Russians have always attached great importance to physical health. Four months later, Maksim managed to steal Galina's heart at gym class, if it could still be called heart stealing since Maksim was the third person Galina had dated at school. While Maksim was floating on air and fooling himself, his subconscious was full of hatred and anger. But he was in love with Galina.

Maksim wanted to marry Galina and introduce her to his mother.

Galina's mother invited Maksim over for dinner, and he gladly accepted. Galina's house was a small apartment with two rooms and a living room. Galina was fortunate because she didn't have to live in crowded dormitories called *kommunalka*, like others did. So, her home was a luxurious one in this respect.

Two months after they met, Maksim felt that Darya had considered him seriously. So, when Maksim was sure about Galina's feelings, he asked Darya to let Galina move to his one-room student house. Darya gave her permission but not because she was fond of Maksim but because it would be better for Galina's mental health to be away from their home.

When the young couple began living in the same house, Maksim changed. Whenever Galina approached him, he turned away from her. And whenever she said, "You don't love me anymore. We should just be friends," he would just say, "Come off it!"

After a while, Maksim began treating Galina just as a sexual object, and instead of loving and caressing her, he was just enacting his sexual fantasies on her. She complied with his requests even if they were painful. He kept saying, "Just this once," but his requests were endless. He continuously dominated Galina to do what he wanted. He also forced her to drink alcohol so that he could achieve his goal.

"Unrestricted sexual satisfaction does not attain love. Instead, love attains sexual satisfaction and even learning the sexual technique."

Erich Fromm

Galina physically submitted to Maksim. He was sure that she was deeply in love with him and that she couldn't live without him.

A week before the New Year, Maksim did not come to home at night without telling Galina. The next day, he was not at the school, either.

Galina started to look for him at police stations and hospitals.

When he came home the day after, the scent of alcohol filled the house as soon as he was inside. He threw himself on the bed without saying anything and passed out. He was unconscious and didn't feel it when Galina undressed him and found a long, black hair between his thigh and balls. Galina packed her stuff in tears and left the house.

It was a very interesting situation. Maksim did not offer any explanation to Galina and did not go to Galina's house.

When they ran across each other at school, Maksim pretended not to see her.

Galina couldn't accept what had happened. She felt so worthless. She didn't understand why Maksim was so distant and ignoring her after he had reached spiritual and physical satisfaction.

A couple of months later, the rumor was that Maksim got engaged and his fiancee was pregnant. He was going to be a father. When she got pregnant, he told her that it was too early to have a child and that they should graduate first; she was devastated.

She felt worthless and incompetent.

When she saw Maksim's fiancee at the university, she fell to pieces once again. She was younger and more beautiful than this woman. Then, she started to investigate his fiancee. When she found out that the woman was not wealthy, she was again shocked. She had been thinking that Maksim left her for money. It was really impossible for her to understand why she had been dumped.

"Psychopaths have no conscience and they don't feel empathy, guilt or faithfulness to anyone but themselves."

Paul Babiak and Robert Hare

The feeling of worthlessness and incompetence grew. Galina began to see herself as a good-for-nothing creature. Her mother was aware of her situation and she decided to take her to see a psychiatrist. The doctor diagnosed her with major depression and started treatment.

Medicine was helping Galina, and she was slowly pulling herself together. She decided to live her life and make the most of its beauty and blessings. She thought that she should not be afraid of life and that she should be brave. She gave up the idea of committing suicide.

"Often the test of courage is not to die but to live."

Vittorio Alfieri

Because of this affective disorder, Galina had affairs with her classmates who showed her some interest, with her unemployed alcoholic neighbor, and even with her teachers.

When Galina graduated, she became a person with no direction who couldn't see and solve her own problems. How she would be out of this tight corner? What would she do? What would be her goal?

Turkish companies were winning contracts in Russia, and private hospitals began to employ Turkish translators. Patient care departments of many private hospitals published job ads for translators. Galina was accepted for the job at her first application. That cheered her up, and she felt lucky. A doctor attended her job interview and decided to hire her.

When Turkish foremen and coordinators brought workers to the hospital for examination, Galina completed all paperwork and referred them to a physician, listening to the complaints of patients and translating them to physicians.

Galina looked like a happy and self-confident woman. She spent her salary on skin care and clothing and frequently mentioned that life was so empty but joyous as well.

Galina woke up early one morning, called Olga, and told her to pick her up in a certain address. Olga was tired of picking her up in different addresses during the week.

"According to Freud, satisfaction of all instinctual desires without restriction will provide mental health and happiness. However, clinical facts show that women and men who pursue sexual satisfaction throughout their lives without any boundary cannot find happiness and mostly suffer from neurotic conflicts and diseases."

Erich Fromm

Olga decided to take Galina for a contagious disease test. Galina's blood test came up clean.

Olga loved Galina so much and didn't want to give up on her. She had been trying her best to make Galina come to her senses. Olga knew that if she didn't help her and left her, she would eternally have a guilty conscience. The solution was to talk to Galina's mother, Darya. When she told Galina about her plan, Galina promised to pull herself together, which convinced Olga.

"If we underestimate a person's self-respect in their connection with society when we approach them and cause them to put away their hope to succeed, discourage them and conclude that they will be of no use, then we cannot feel justified because we will be the source of that person's suffering."

Alfred Adler

One day, Galina was waiting for Olga for the birthday party of the founder of the hospital, Dr. Sergey Valantinov. She looked at the mirror and sighed. "If I had a child, everything would be different."

It is not necessary to get married to have a child. Marriage is a bygone anyhow. And what's more, the state encouraged giving birth to address the population decrease due to alcohol and paid no attention if the mother was married or not. As a matter of fact, the mothers received state support even if there is no known father of the child. She thought her mother would not be angry if she would have a child. Her mother was married, so what?

That night, Galina was looking around to find someone to get pregnant by. When she regained consciousness, she saw that Dr. Dimitri was getting dressed. As she was going downstairs to the restaurant of the hotel with him for breakfast, she remembered that he was married. She muttered, "He had already made a choice when he hired me."

Dr. Dimitri rented a house for Galina, and she lived there. She was not tempted to have an affair with someone else, not because of her faithfulness to Dr. Dimitri but for fear of losing her job. And she didn't want to live under the same roof as her alcoholic father again.

Dr. Dimitri's interest in her was almost everlasting. Because she was feeling herself incompetent and worthless, she was not aware of her own value. She ascribed his devotion to other things. Galina made him spend money on her, she wanted him to take her out... In short, Galina was a woman without any expense. He must have rented the house not because he cherished her but because staying at a hotel was expensive.

When they visited her hometown, Nijniy Novgorod, due to her aunt's death, she told him that she liked this city too much and wanted to stay there for a week.

During this one-week vacation, Galina convinced her cousin Svetlana to go to a bar despite the funeral. That night, Dr. Dimitri couldn't reach Galina.

"The best time for people to know each other is just before they break up."
Dostoyevsky

Under the influence of alcohol, Galina woke up in another bed that morning.

Dr. Dimitri put Galina's belongings into cardboard boxes, gave them to Olga, and kicked Galina out without even waiting for her return.

He didn't even consider something unexpected and terrible might have happened to her. That same flesh and same voice had been boring him for months. For the last couple of weeks, he had been feeling much negativity toward her. His intuitions had not misled him to date.

Galina deserved to be written off. His pride couldn't stand her anymore; she was always late to work at the hospital and always had her own way. He fired her from work and removed her from his life in a single stroke and without even talking to her.

Dr. Dimitri never thought of having Galina treated for alcohol or hysteria; he never wanted to help her.

*

When Dr. Dimitri decided to break up with her, Galina decided to do some soul-searching. But she gave up soul-searching because she wanted to be with men. Then, she listened to her inner voice again. Her inner voice was telling her that she was letting men take advantage of her. She had the same feeling of being taken advantage of every time she woke up in some man's bed. The compliments men gave her were nothing but a trick to have sex with her. She always hoped that a man's interest in her or devotion to her would never come to an end. She thought men's behaviors told her that she owned them, and her hysterical acts would make them man stay with her forever.

"Look into the depths of your own soul and learn first to know yourself, then you will understand why this illness was bound to come upon you and perhaps you will thenceforth avoid falling ill."

Sigmund Freud

She kept thinking that she was fooling herself by doing the same thing repeatedly. Even the slightest possibility that the man might belong to her eventually and that the compliments will never end was enough for her to be a fool, to deceive herself. She was always aware of her partners' cheating, but every time she had allowed them to cheat on her. No one would deceive her and cheat on her if she didn't approve or allow this.

"The easiest thing of all is to deceive one's self; for what a man wishes, he generally believes to be true."

Demosthenes

When she was considering these facts, she thought about Dr. Dimitri's wife, Ekaterina. His wife always humiliated him because his family was poor. She embarrassed him in front of his friends and treated him as if he was her personal butler. Yes, her wife was beautiful, and he became a partner in the hospital with her money, but her actions had caused him to cheat on her. Dimitri had no other choice. Therefore, Galina had a clean conscience about Dr. Dimitri's wife.

In this context, Galina had taken her affair with Dr. Dimitri for granted. She had never thought that in a bilateral relationship where she wasn't a party, the wrong that both parties do each other only concern those parties. Although Galina thought she was with Dr. Dimitri for the sake of her job and house, the main reason was that she had planned to fight with his wife and get rid of feelings of insecurity regarding her womanhood and personality. In fact, this was a reflection of her childhood desire to take her mother away from her father. What was important in this relationship for Galina was not Dr. Dimitri, with whom she was having an affair, but his wife, Ekaterina.

Dr. Dimitri became closer to Ekaterina as his relationship with Galina continued. On the other hand, being close to Galina was not a pleasure to him anymore but a burden.

He was fed up with his wife's dominance and sought for a safe haven. This haven was Galina. Even though what Galina did have harmed his manhood, his main reason for breaking up with her was his fear of losing Ekatarina's support. On one hand was the dominant and humiliating Ekaterina, and the tender and sexy Galina on the other. He was like a child who gets bored of a dominant mother at home, runs away to play and then comes back again.

"A man is happy so long as he chooses to be happy."
Aleksandr Solzhenitsyn

*

After being fired and kicked out from her apartment, Galina moved to Olga's home.

Galina wanted to find a new job now. She was also in search of a rich husband to have a laid-back life. But it was not easy to find a rich man to marry in Russia. Rich men were scarce, and there were so many in the hunt.

So many had lost their jobs after the dissolution of the Soviet Union. Therefore, rich men in Russia were generally engaged in monkey business. Middle class had been destroyed. Only the poor had remained.

Galina decided to give up the idea of finding a rich husband for a while and was urgently trying to find a job. She thought should not place a strain on Olga and must cover her daily needs.

One night, Olga and Galina visited Olga's stepfather to ask him to find a job for Galina. Olga's stepfather, Vladimir, had served as a diplomat in numerous capitals for years. Now he was a board member of a defence industry company.

Vladimir took Galina's phone number that night and told her that he would call her soon. A few days later, Vladimir called and invited her for an interview.

She was happy because she thought she would be employed by Vladimir's company, so she was there on time.

Vladimir was a typical Russian. He cut a long story short. He told Galina that SVR was looking for a Turkish-speaking person and that he would give her a reference if she was interested.

This kind of a job had never occurred to Galina but as if she had no expectations from life, she accepted it without a second thought and said she would appreciate it very much. Then, she gave her resume to Vladimir.

She did not expect him to call her back soon, and she kept reading job adverts. She applied to a transportation company in Turkey and got a job as a translator. Galina was really lucky.

Then, she received a phone call from Vladimir about the other job, which she had already completely forgotten. As she was not happy with her job because it was not a corporate company and they were not paying her salary regularly, Vladimir's call made her so happy.

Vladimir told her that they would call her for an interview soon and if the interview went well, official procedures would begin immediately.

At the interview, Galina understood that she would be working in the field.

A few weeks later, news came that she got the job. She immediately called Vladimir to thank him for his support and invited him over for dinner. She didn't have enough money to have dinner outside, so she was going to entertain him, including Olga and her mother, at her place.

She was so surprised about getting the job because she knew that it was impossible to find a job in the public sector without bribing someone in Russia. Galina didn't have any money to bribe Vladimir anyhow. She thought she would thank him in some other way. She had more than two bottles of wine at the dinner, but he did not have sex with her. The reason was not Olga. He simply did not want to have sex with her.

"If all you have is a hammer, everything looks like a nail."

Abraham Maslow

*

Galina invited Olga and her mother over dinner to thank her. Olga glanced at the dinner table and saw the rich spread. There were even smoked meat and caviar canapes.

"You shouldn't have!" Olga said to Galina and Darya.

Darya started the conversation by telling Galina's childhood memories. Then, Darya stood up and told them that she wanted to make an important speech:

"One night, Santa Claus knocked on the door of a young man. When the young man opened the door, Santa Claus said, 'I will give you three options tonight and you can only select one of them.'

The young man excitedly said, 'I am all ears!'

Santa Claus continued, 'The first option is five million rubles. The second option is happiness, and third one is a good friend.'

The young man thought for a short while and replied, 'I choose the third option, because a good friend brings happiness and money along.'"

"To friendship," said Galina. The three of them clinked their glasses and sipped their wines.

Darya left the table to go to sleep. Galina's father, Boris, who was drunk as usual, followed her to bedroom.

Olga looked into Galina's eyes, reached out and said, "Galiniçka, I want something from you but don't say no right away!"

"Go ahead, Olga! Why would I say no?"

"I would like to take you to Ms. Yulya on Friday. She is a very good psychologist and might help you leave bad days behind! We can go together and get her advice."

"Is that what you want to do? Of course, we can."

In the psychologist's office, the secretary looked at them and asked, "Galina Ivanova?"

"Yes," Galina replied.

Olga said, "I'm a close friend. I also wanted to see her."

"She will call you," said the secretary and went back to work.

Galina was then called to Yulya's room. "Hello," said Yulya, "please take a seat." She glanced around and shyly sat down. "Would you like to have coffee?" asked Yulya.

"Drip coffee if you have," said Galina.

Galina began to tell her about herself, but Yulya interrupted her a couple of minutes later by saying, "It would be easier for us to find a solution if we talk about the events and our feelings truly." Then, she continued to listen to her attentively and take notes.

> *"It takes two to speak the truth: one to speak, and another to hear."*
> *Henry David Thoreau*

Yulya observed Galina as if she was a guinea pig. She never interrupted Galina other than asking a question. Yulya took a napkin from the drawer and handed it to Galina.

When Galina finished talking, Yulya took a sip of water from her glass, turned over the paper on which she took her notes and began her assessment. Galina told her so many things that Yulya took two pages of notes.

"Your life is full of black and white only," said Yulya. "You don't have any shade of gray anymore. You have what is called bipolar disorder."

"Like all or nothing?" asked Galina.

Yulya nodded, "Yes! It is always either yes or no for you! For example, you think you are either valuable or not, successful or not. There is no in between for you. Your life is a complete dilemma, and you always place yourself on the negative side. First, you need to learn not to accept a bipolar life. This is a fundamental type of thought disorder. Don't ever judge and blame yourself! By always blaming yourself, you have begun to believe that all negativity around you are stemming from you. I will not repeat what I will say now. So, I want you to listen very carefully and understand it thoroughly."

Galina looked into Yulya's eyes and nodded.

Yulya continued, "OK! The feeling of guilt cannot fix the past. Therefore, it is a useless feeling. If we have a time machine, then it might be useful one. Then you can go back to your past and correct your mistakes.

Because of your feeling of guilt, you are unable to tolerate yourself. First of all, you need to learn to be tolerant of yourself. Guilt spoils the moment you live and makes you concerned about your future. Guilt makes you condemn yourself in your subconscious and you may even hate yourself. If it is repeated, these feelings gradually stiffen. When you think of negativities, you ignore your own values. Your experiences cannot only be negative. There are definitely positive ones, too. You have to think them over."

She added, "I also took a note of how you have placed yourself in the center of the world."

"It's not like that, actually."

"I think it is. You have taken everything personally and made everything about you. You identify and associate everything with yourself. For example, when something was lost at your office, you were worried if they will suspect you of stealing it. This might just your imagination, but before you know it, it may reflect on the universe and become true. Such negative thoughts may trigger distorted interactions. Therefore, you should not have negative thoughts about yourself and happenings. Negative thoughts reflect on you, your actions, and ultimately your life and come true."

"Yes! From time to time it happens."

"You think everybody in your life thinks and decides like you. The fact is that humans are different from each other. Just take finger prints for example. The way people think, and their thoughts are also different. You have always assumed that you can read others' minds and concluded that they are unhappy or ascribed them other negativities. Thus, your relationships have resulted in tragedy."

"Yes! You are right!"

"You always make the same big mistake. When you have the chance to dialogue with others and deliberate over something, you prefer a monologue and cut off communication with them. It is highly likely for you to be introverted."

Lifting her eyebrows, Yulya set her eyes on Galina.

"Now and then I become introverted or I think I am."

"Single-sided thoughts make you become more introverted. Talk to people. If there is a problem, find out what it is. Establishing dialogue is the first step. You cannot know whether your mistakes are really mistakes or not. A mistake is a real mistake only if it is fatal or unrecoverable. Otherwise, it is not a mistake but a preference. It's what you prefer to do! You have chosen to act that way and acted. You may have learned your lesson not to make the same or a similar choice.

When you think negatively or blame yourself, there is a formula to find a way out.

Talk to yourself! Say, 'I am not a bad person even if others think so. What they think is irrelevant. I have good sides like being warm-hearted, beautiful, and benevolent. My upsides outweigh my downsides. I am not desperate, but it is true that sometimes I find myself stuck in a difficult situation, but I will overcome this.

Everybody acts as if there is clear evidence about me, as if they have asked 100 people and 99 of them spoke ill of me. No, I'm not that negative person! Nobody can judge me to be so! Even I cannot judge myself. This is not a courtroom, but my negative thoughts try to pull me toward a courtroom as if it is the date of my trial. I am not a judge! Neither you, nor them! But even judges also misjudge. People who do 30 years in prison may be proven innocent after 30 years and be acquitted. Only someone who lives what I have lived can judge me.'

Tell your inner critic firmy, 'This is not a court. I don't care about anyone! What would happen to me? Am I gonna die? Leave the courtroom! Stop living in trial! Enjoy your life! Listen to music you like or do something that would make you let yourself go!'

Try this formula for a few weeks. If you feel relieved, it means you are making progress!"

"What should I do if they don't help?"

"Then you have to try the second formula. You must confront your fears. For example, your most destructive emotion is feeling worthless. Write down *worthless* on your identity card with a pencil. Hold your identity card from time to time and look at it for a couple of weeks. Even if you feel that you are worthless, you will see that it is not the end. Negative thoughts are like spider webs. If you face yourself and accept your realities, you can pierce through the web like strong bugs, and your negative thoughts cannot take root in your mind."

"If you want to get rid of your concerns, then accept that you may experience your biggest fear."

Socrates

"If you do not practice them rationally, decisively, and strongly, and you give up, you can never get out of depression as a result of helplessness and hopelessness. Something you do when you are depressed will lead to a new one and cause a chain reaction. You'll keep coming here, listening to the same advice in different ways.

In addition, having an affair with a married man will not be coincidence anymore but a habit. So, don't do this mistake again and keep being the 'second woman'! You have no right to do this to yourself! You really don't! Why? Because you are in no position to stand the stress that will be imposed on you anymore. Resolve to not have an affair with a married man from now on and stick to it.

Affairs with married men or one-night stands will make it difficult for you to commit yourself to a single man because you will be used to changing partners. Breaking up with someone will be easy for you, and you will lose the depth of your relationship, and it will go on just for the sake of sex. Which is what happening now, right?"

"Unfortunately," said Galina. "What happens if my relationships are just for sex for a little while longer?"

"Here you go! Never-ending sexual urge is an indicator of an addiction. Therefore, you cannot experience the romance you aspire, and it is the sign of superficiality. When you get addicted to sex, then it will not matter to you with whom you do it, under which circumstances, or how. When you are not satisfied emotionally, it becomes meaningless and your relationships become superficial. Your inner peace will be harmed, and you'll feel worthless."

Galina was intrigued. "What kind of an addiction is this? Is it something like drug addiction?"

Yulya replied, "Yes. Drug addicts want to find drugs no matter what it costs and no matter where it ends. They are not able to think what will happen after. Let me exemplify the reflection of this addiction on you. A swindler keeps thinking how to swindle someone and get his money. Nothing else matters for him. In your case, you keep thinking of having sex, nothing else. With whom, where, or how, these don't matter for you. You spend your energy and strength to have sex, that's all!"

When the session was over, Olga stood up and before entering Yulya's office, she asked Galina, "How did it go?"

"Helpful," said Galina.

Olga quickly entered Yulya's office. She was anxious to hear Yulya's assessment of her friend.

"She will pull herself together if she listens to me," said Yulya. She feels insecure, and she makes wrong decisions for the sake of momentary pleasure. She fears loneliness.

The density of her negative thoughts causes an excessive need to have balance. In other words, they have turned into inner reactions. Due to her inner reactions, she always wants more than one person in her life. Whenever someone breaks up with her, she wants to be with someone else because she is afraid to be alone. She keeps thinking of all those bad things that happened to her, and instead of focusing on other things, she prefers to ease herself with alcohol.

Interfering with her flirtatious nature will not be fruitful. Galina is intrinsically a flirty woman. She likes to flirt with men. Her flirtatious nature may change only if she can find a man who would make her feel completely secure.

She thinks one-night stands may lead to serious relationships, so she goes to bed with any man she meets because some of her affairs have started this way and, considering her nature, they have lasted rather long.

Whenever a man falls all over her, she tends to be deceived easily because she feels worthless and she thinks having sex with him may lead to a better relationship. She likes to be taken care of. She wants her body to be owned by a man. And when a man owns her body, she mistakenly perceives it as he also owns her soul.

The feeling of worthlessness leads one to unconditional submission. She thinks she will be valued this way."

Yulya stopped talking for a moment. She was about to stand up but continued to talk as she remembered something. "Apart from the feeling of worthlessness, she also has a self-confidence issue. To conceal her insecurity, she wants to seduce men and prove herself to herself and others, so she tries to challenge everyone. Her quest for the love from her father that she never had underlies this. She also cannot forget her mother's depression throughout her marriage. It is intriguing that when I asked her if she ever tried to attract others' attention or stand out when she was a child, she said yes.

Many of our problems are hereditary, and their symptoms are seen in childhood. She will recover in time. Please continue to support her. Don't leave her alone. Give her small but meaningful gifts. Invite her over for coffee or dinner. Never forget that one's best psychiatrist is her best friend. If I tell her everything at once as a psychiatrist, she might react. This is why I need your help to tell her what I have told you. Thus, you may help her to understand what's in her subconscious."

Olga left Yulya's room. She lovingly smiled at Galina. When Yulya saw them off, she gave them one last advice. "Yes, young ladies. What we have talked about is not important. What's important is shaping our lives by putting them into practice."

When they were going down the stairs, Galina said, "Thank you very much, Ol. I will begin to follow Ms. Yulya's advice today."

Olga looked at Galina. "I want you to be happy."

"Wishing others to be happy is a virtue."

Erich Fromm

*

Galina was all beaten up because of intensive trainings and studying. She liked field trainings more than theoretical courses.

Courses like history of SVR, intelligence and importance of intelligence, intelligence gathering methods, counter intelligence, analysis and assessment, intelligence services of target countries, examples of side changing in history, tracking, tracking avoidance, using weapons, using and detecting monitoring and surveillance devices, infiltration, engaging, fake character bibliography (mask life story), fast disguise, driving under pressure, and deceiving the lie detector, interrogation techniques, and methods of answering in interrogations have excited her attention.

Galina was sure that she would be appointed to Turkey next. And she was right. Galina was very happy. She had a big deal of knowledge about Turkey and Turks when she was studying Turkish. She had solidified many of these information in Crimea during her first mission. She had no doubt about it. She would succeed in Turkey.

But the assignment letter was a disappointment for her. Galina was not appointed as a diplomat at the embassy, contrary to her expectation. The assignment letter stated that she was appointed as a project assistant at the Main Office of United Nations High Commissioner for Refugees (UNHCR) in Turkey (Ankara).

Galina's only concern was not having diplomatic immunity. This kind of assignment was considered illegal in intelligence language and being assigned as a diplomat was considered legal. Moreover, the penalty for espionage was really severe in Turkey.

For a moment she thought she shouldn't accept the job at the agency.

"The experimenter who does not know what he is looking for will not understand what he finds."

Claude Bernard

But it was too late. What was done was done, and she had to keep in step with the new circumstances.

SVR had written a professional application letter for Galina to be accepted for the job and sent it from Galina's personal e-mail address and also by post. When Galina was pulling herself together, she thought that she was accepted by UNHCR mainly because of the clandestine activities at the humanitarian aid institutions in Crimea. Then she thought, "There may be some people from SVR."

Galina requested information from officials regarding how she came to be accepted through internal correspondence and regarding the details of the correspondence—about herself, dates, and similar details.

Even so, she was trying to be pleased. At least she would be working outside of the hierarchy of the embassy, the intelligence base (*rezidentura*) stationed at the embassy, and she would not be working under the *rezident*, who was the head of this service, and will not be subject to the strict rules of this structure.

"Maybe they are trying to place some agents who would not be associated with the embassy," she thought. "I wish I would be assigned to work under the assistant *rezident* responsible for sabotaging railroads and highways," she murmured.

She was briefed and instructed and ready to go.

Her targets were the senior staff and diplomats at the UN, senior diplomats from other countries she would meet at various events, and faculty members at the Institute of Social Sciences of Ankara University, where she will be applying for her master's degree, who consult with the Turkish government. Her mission was to establish intimacy with such people, find out their weaknesses, engage them to work for Russia, and establish an intelligence network.

Galina's workload was rather dense. Normally an illegal agent should only mark and engagement were done by legal agents, but now Galina had to do everything and undertake all risks. Sometimes the corporate office spurned the security of the operation, requesting the impossible, and sometimes even demasked the small fish. Were they demasking Galina on purpose? Was there someone, a traitor, a mole, at the corporate office, sabotaging and giving agents difficult missions that were sure failures?

Galina's other target was to engage enemy agencies' officials and provide them with manipulative information, with approval from the head office. The aim was to misguide them by telling them that they have many spies among them, adding to the paranoia of enemy agencies and making them inoperable.

Apart from these, keeping track of those who were notified by the head office and supporting blackmail, entrapment, and persuasion operations of the head office when required were also her duties.

Galina always thought she was commissioned in Turkey because of her fluent Turkish and her success in the field and trainings. But this was not the real reason. The most determinative criterion for being commissioned in a critical country like Turkey where secret services were heavily active was her awareness of Russia's emperorship and superpower and her patriotism. Vladimir had told her to reply to the interview questions in this respect and use the sentence "I am always proud of my country for it has 11 time zones and the largest acreage" and the phrase "Russia is my soul."

Another reason for Galina's appointment for a difficult mission was her love for daring ventures.

Commissioning an agent who was not devoted to their country abroad meant invitation made by services to make the enemy services to try to convince the agent to change sides.

Ankara

Within three days, Galina found a beautiful house that made her happy. According to the rules of the service, she should not hire a cleaner from outside. It has fallen to lot. She only made the rough cleaning of the house at the end of the first day.

She was requested to spend Friday getting to know Ankara better. The weather was warmer than Moscow, but she still wanted to wear her flamboyant fur. In principle, wearing attention-grabbing attire was forbidden but only when working.

Galina was walking around the Tunali Hilmi Street, and she saw a poodle. The dog resembled Richard's dog. Richard was a British citizen in charge of foreign nongovernmental organizations in Crimea.

Galina was an expert in cats and dogs. She was a good dog trainer, especially in toilet training. She was trained by SVR about cat and dog breeds and their characteristics so that she could get close to targets owning cats and dogs and enter their homes.

In Crimea, Galina was very accustomed to eating *cig borek*, a deep-fried wafer-thin dough with raw minced meat filling. So, one of the first things she tried to find in Ankara was *cig borek*. There were generally patisseries, soup restaurants, and kebab shops on Tunali Hilmi Street, but there was no *cig borek* shop on sight.

She also did not test whether she was being followed or not. She might have been followed. But she wasn't working, so a test was not necessary. She was acting normal.

While looking at the showcases, Galina was repeating in her mind the fake story created about her past. She graduated from the Department of Turkish, worked at a hospital, transportation company, textile company, and finally at a certified translation office. Talking about SVR was off-limits. In the meantime, she had done her master's degree on social policies in the Faculty of World Politics of Lomonosof, Moscow State University. Her thesis was on globalized capitalism and its impact on the development of peoples. Since she had worked at a translation office for a long time, she was concentrated on details proving she had worked at a translation office.

These evidences included the following: photomontages showing her with people who have worked at the translation company in those years, phone numbers of those who have worked at the translation company, the business card that the restaurant near the translation company had printed for reservations and which she kept in her wallet. Moreover, Turkish translations made at the translation company at the time when Galina worked there had been copied by hackers and transferred to Galina's computer. Galina just had to read them, be informed about the translations, and memorize the titles of translated texts and some unusual their parts. Galina studied the details such as the names of her friends and translation subjects on which they were experts. She also didn't forget to bring the photos she had with her friends when working at the humanitarian aid institution in Crimea and the bulletins they had prepared.

In fact, her story was not complete fiction. The translation company and a master's degree were added to her real life. Truths were included in the lies so that she would not be demasked.

Galina was unavoidably afraid of being demasked.

...a lie which is all a lie may be met and fought with outright; but a lie which is part a truth is a harder matter to fight."

Alfred Lord Tennyson

A Few Months After Arrival in Ankara

Galina had successfully met with her targets one by one and established relationships with them. She had also been spending two hours a day at doctorate courses that began in February.

Prof. Dr. Hilmi Dagdeviren was her instructor on Turkish foreign policy. Galina successfully discussed the views of Turkey on minorities in Russia (particularly Muslim and Turkish-origin communities or communities related to Turks), red lines of Turkey regarding the Armenian Issue and the Nagorno-Karabakh issue, and whether there would be detente in these matters with mutual compromises.

Professor Hilmi was a tight-lipped man, but he shared his opinions with Galina, not because she was a beautiful woman but because she was a determined and eager student. Nobody was aware of Turkey's future yet.

After he had shared these with Galina, Professor Hilmi smelled a rat and got suspicious. He called his classmate, Mr. Ahmet, and asked him to investigate Galina to see whether her interest was innocent, or she was trying to collect intelligence. Mr. Ahmet was a high-level officer at MIT (National Intelligence Service–Turkish Intelligence). Mr. Ahmet met Professor Hilmi at his doctorate courses and they had been close friends since.

Before leaving Moscow, Galina had been told by Vitali, her manager in Crimea, that there was a prejudice against those from the Soviet geography and that she should hurry to complete her mission. Galina was afraid to be considered unsuccessful and called back, so she was in a hurry. Her precipitousness and impatience have precluded her professionalism.

Upon the request of Professor Hilmi, an investigation was commenced on Galina; she was being investigated thoroughly.

Galina's contacts at the institution she worked and her discussions with professors in the university made it necessary to keep a close watch on her.

Thereupon, Mr. Nihat from MIT's Counterintelligence Department decided to bring Galina under control and called the personnel he trusted most, Teoman, to his room. Teoman memorized every word that came out of Mr. Nihat's mouth and told him that he would report all details to Mr. Nihat before leaving the room.

Teoman examined the file as soon as he went back to his desk. He took some notes and interviewed Professor Hilmi and other faculty members in the university. Some of the other faculty members stated that Galina was not interested in their courses; she did not ask questions, she just took notes, and she even wasn't involved in discussions. It was obvious that Galina took interest only in Professor Hilmi's course. This might have been a coincidence. Galina probably liked Professor Hilmi's course or felt a closeness to him. But when it comes to intelligence, opinions and actions evolved inversely.

Teoman investigated Galina's relationships and contacts in detail but couldn't find any suspicious relationship or any contact with the employees of the embassy.

Teoman examined Galina's photo and tried to build her profile. Galina had protruding cheeks, and her face was square. A typology was revealed for her, with her small and pointed chin, upright eyebrows, thin lips, a big mouth, narrow forehead, a thin and long nose, and upright ears. Teoman revealed that a person with these facial features is pitiless and rough, untrustworthy, cunning, highly creative, tight-lipped, likes to work solo, has a good command of technical matters, uses her left brain efficiently, and very influential. Apart from these, the traces and lines on her face, her hair, beauty spots, dimples, teeth, and other organs should be closely examined to completely determine her personality.

Teoman and his team were waiting in a car at a nearby location to Galina's house to monitor and spy on her in the wee hours of the morning. Her house was on the street. This made it difficult for him and his team to keep tabs on her. The team was focused on the street door of her building. Seven persons came out of the door, but not Galina.

Teoman and his team didn't have a decent breakfast. "If we knew she would be this late, we would have had a nice breakfast," they said and laughed. It was a very busy month for them.

Galina finally came out of the house. She was walking down the street and looked like a model on a catwalk with her dark hair, green eyes, wheat-white colored velvety skin, and long legs.

"She is very beautiful," they said but said nothing more because they had female members in the team. They did not indulge in male bonding. In fact, there was a lot to talk about!

Galina's legs were 5 to 6 cm. longer that those of Turkish women. When Galina's mother, Darya, was born, instead of looking at Darya's face, Darya's father uncovered the towel on Darya's legs and said, "*Slava Bogu naşa paroda.*" Thank God she took after us. Darya's mother was a Kazan Tatar.

When Galina was born, Darya's father combined the proverb "Scratch the Russian and you find a Tatar" with another proverb "When a Tatar was born, a Jew has died" and came up with a nonsensical joke—"When Galina was born, you find Vodka." During the celebrations, he drank *samagon*, a homemade, high-alcohol vodka, for three days and fell into a coma.

At the end of days-long investigation, nothing suspicious have been found about Galina except her discussions with the faculty members in the university.

Upon the request of MIT, the Director of Social Sciences Institute has notified all Turkish faculty members and instructors to inform MIT regarding specific questions asked by foreign students about matters related to national security and politics. Teoman was trying to find out what was Galina up to.

Galina has tried to contact John Brown, an American citizen and chairman of the institution where Galina worked, a couple of times but could not cross the formality wall.

Galina had to engage John at all costs.

John Brown was a meticulous manager. He was reading every report thoroughly, assessing them, taking notes, and regardless of his workload, querying the experts who wrote the reports as soon as possible. John was also a very active man. He always showed up at embassy cocktails and attended all symposia held in Ankara and Istanbul related to his field of activity either as a speaker or panel moderator. When he wasn't playing the role of a speaker, he always sat in the front row and continuously took notes.

Galina decided to establish rapport with John during the celebration dinner given every Easter. She had been applying a facial mask every day for a week, so she did not to look tired at Easter dinner. She had also been working on questions and answers.

Three long tables were prepared for the party. John was sitting in the middle of the first table, facing other tables.

It was unlikely for Galina to sit at the first table because her seat was at the third one. John gave a speech early in the night and then sat down with applause.

Galina did not want to stumble today. She began thinking fast. John was going out to make a call with his mobile phone, then he would come back and greet the personnel before sitting down.

Galina sensed that this could not be the way to get close to him.

Galina has attended the dinner in a very assertive and low-cut black dress. She took the stage with her friends at every song but couldn't attract John's attention. For the first time in her life, she was unable to attract the attention of a man she wanted.

Galina counted the drinks John had had like she counted the number of remaining bullets in the charger, trying to see whether he was drunk.

Time was getting shorter and John might not stay untill the end of the night. Live music was about to end. It was 11:45 pm.

When Galina stood up to go to toilet, she came eye to eye with the man on the stage. He announced that there will be five competitions and five prizes will be given in every competition.

When Galina came back from the toilet, she came eye to eye with the presenter again. Instead of the competition to find the whistle behind the man in the middle of the stage, the presenter was still looking at Galina. Galina approached the stage and called the presenter. Everybody was drunk and they didn't notice Galina's conversation with the presenter.

"May I ask a favor?" Galina said in fluent Turkish.

The presenter was surprised. "Sure!"

Galina continued, "Would you please match me with Mr. John for one of the competitions? Because my unit manager is not very happy with me. If I meet him, maybe I will not be discharged, and I may treat you with a coffee later."

The presenter's eyes glowed and grinned from ear to ear. "With pleasure," he said.

Competitors have formed a circle on the stage. Roland, a Swiss citizen, was standing in the middle of the stage and trying to find the whistle attached to the back of his jacket and blown by the person standing right behind him. But he was drunk and could not find the whistle. The presenter grew impatient and gave Roland a cue with his eyes and lifted his eyebrows to let him understand that the whistle was on his back and Roland has found the whistle.

Everybody had great fun, and even though the competition was not funny, they laughed like crazy under the influence of alcohol.

The presenter was so excited and announced the picture drawing competition even though it should be the last competition. He announced in English that he was going to invite two ladies and two men for this competition. The humming stopped immediately.

He selected John and Galina as the first couple and Araz from Iran and Selina from Greece as the second couple.

The competition was about drawing a picture which emphasizes the meaning and importance of the date in just a minute. John, Galina, Selina, and Araz hurriedly started to draw pictures with pastels.

At the end of the period, John and Galina showed the picture they drew on the cardboard. It was a display of the sun with stick men under it. On the cardboard of Araz and Selina, there were seven circles drawn side-by-side and eggs patterned with lines.

The pictures were really funny. The winners of the competition were John and Galina for sure. The presenter handed the first prize to Galina. Galina turned to John and said, "We must share this Mr. John."

"Of course," said John, and they picked the champagne glasses and popped up the bottle.

Being under the influence of alcohol he consumed all night, John invited Galina to his table. They sat side by side with and stroke up a conversation.

"To your happiness," said Galina cosily and raised her glass in a toast. Galina told John that they stir the champagne with the metal around the cork before drinking in Russia to degas it. This way drinking it was more joyous.

John said he normally prefers wine and whenever he drinks champagne after wine, he gets very drunk. Galina was about to say something, but she saw John look at his watch.

Galina thought she still could not produce the effect she wanted and said, "Let me tell you about my memory regarding champagne."

Slightly cross-eyed John looked at her and smiled as if saying, "Okay."

Galina thought she should make a fast move. She understood again that there is long way ahead to be very close with John. She decided to cut the long story short and continued, "When I was a second-year student in the university, me and my two girlfriends have drunk four bottles of champagnes in the amuse-ment park in Gorky Park in Moscow. We were really drunk. Then I decided to make the score of the year at the box machine. I envisioned my ex-boyfriend's picture on the sandbag and punched it with all my strength. Even so, I only scored 30 points. Then my girlfriends started punching. They have scored 25 points at the most. As we kept punching the sandbag, three young men came by. They were drinking beer. They watched as and laughed. I turned to them and said, "C'mon! Let's compete!"

"Okay," they said, "What's the bet?"

I bit my lip and said, "How about a blowjob?"

John had an epiphany and thought of something that didn't occur to him before. Sex! Everybody at the institution was gossiping that John is not inter-ested in women so he might be gay.

30

John curiously asked, "Then what happened?" "We lost" said Galina. John started to laugh and lifted his thumb. It was obvious that big and arrogant workaholic has liked it. Galina continued, "But we didn't do it!"

John cut a long story short and invited Galina to a bar at the end of the street where he said the music is beautiful. Galina said she doesn't have time, but she also doesn't want to offend him and accepted the offer. Galina was curious about the expression that would appear on John's face when she pretended to pull herself back a little after her story.

"I don't have much time either," John replied in a diplomatic manner. What John loved most in Turkey was diplomatic answers that Turks give.

Galina went to the bar by taxi and John took his own car.

They couldn't find a table to sit at in the bar. So, they decided to stand in the bistro. The waiter brought their drinks and when Galina was about to make a toast, John kissed her on the lips. Galina was without a man for months. She didn't want to be seen as she didn't want it and put her hand on John's face and continued to kiss him emotionally.

She said, "Take it easy cowboy!"

Galina thought she was an expert on passionate sex. John was indifferent to women after leaving his lover who was hostile to men and therefore had no orgasm. His affair was finished two months ago, and Galina was the first woman she had sex since then. In short, fire and gunpowder were together. John was overwhelmed because she made Galina very happy and was feeling like a real man. The feeling of incompetence was the only legacy of her ex-lover Katrina.

Galina's relationship with John was going on behind the closed doors. But John was the only one pleased. Because of the pepper pills that John takes before they make love, Galina was getting up from bed dripping wet. She has never felt this humiliated before. "Bastard! He has sex and sports at the same time." She was so pissed off.

In her relationship with John, Galina was convinced that Americans were not that smart at all. Their working discipline was so strong, that's all.

As John was a workaholic, he was taking all papers and documents to home. But even though the briefcase was bulged, there were not much on his desk. Galina realized that there was a secret place in John's home. One night, she bought some wine from the grocery, filled them into the two-liter bottle and took it to John's place. She said it was a home-made wine.

Before serving it to John, she mixed a special sleeping medicine prepared by SVR in his wine. It was a strong medicine and John should be in sleep for five hours.

First, Galina checked with a detector whether there were hidden cameras in the house or not. It was clean. It was time to find the one in the house, now. Galina finally found the secret case. She needed John's finger to open the case. Galina was prepared. She took his fingerprint with the machine she had in her purse, put it on some kind of a gel and managed to open the safe. She took pictures of everything in the safe.

She didn't examine the documents and photos in the safe. It was forbidden to know the content of the documents and information. Because she should not say anything in an interrogation if she gets caught. These rules were established for this reason. But she took a glance at the documents when she was taking their photos. There was information in the reports regarding the places for humanitarian aid in case of a war in Turkey and in its neighbors, its cost and locations of refugee camps to be established and some maps.

The next day she went to the gym to deliver the microchip to trainer Mariya, who was a Kazakh. But when she arrived there, she found out Mariya had a car accident on her way in. So Mariya would come two hours later.

Galina was always exercising for 45 minutes at the gym. If she stays at the gym for an additional period of one hour and 15 minutes without her trainer Mariya would cause suspicion.

Risking herself was not necessary. So, she decided to keep the microchip full of pictures of documents for two more days. But it was very risky because there was an X-ray device at the entrance of her workplace. Because of the bomb warnings, sometimes the security officer at the door was passing all belongings through the device repeatedly till the X-ray stops beeping. She could dare to take this risk and put the microchip between the bristles of toilet brush next to the toilet bowl at home.

In the evening, she left her office and came to home. The signs she left before leaving the house were intact, so she was sure that nobody entered her home during the day. She checked the microchip. She breathed a sigh of relief, because the chip was there.

The next day she followed the same routine, came back home, checked everything and went to the gym to deliver the microchip. When she saw Mariya, she was so happy as if she saw her mother. He handed over the microchip to Mariya. She felt so relieved.

*

Galina woke up in the middle of the night and decided to sleep on the couch in the living room. Before going to living room, she took a glance at the kitchen table. There were some snacks but she preferred to drink half a glass of water.

When she woke up in the morning, she felt exhausted. For some reason, she was restless. She could make nothing of her dreams, either. She hopped in the shower. She noticed that she run short of refreshing mentholated shower gel. She emptied the remaining gel on her palm. She dabbed the gel on every part of her body equally and rubbed it in. She filled the gel box with some water and shook it. She rubbed the last drops of gel on her hands. She waited for a while, held the shower head, turned on the water and took her shower.

She wrapped towels around her waist and back and went to the kitchen. It occurred to her that she didn't dry her hair and got back to bathroom. Seemingly, mentholated freshness of the gel couldn't make Galina to gather herself up.

While sipping her coffee, she squinted and tried to remember the dream she had at night. In her dream, it was New Year celebrations in Russia. She was missing Russia so much. She was kind of smelling a scent which is a mixture of fresh pine and mandarin her mother bought for New Year.

She made her plans for the night. There was dried fish (taranka) and cold beer in the fridge. She had to dry her hair and shape it with curling iron. "Come on you lazy girl," she said and got up from the table.

She got dressed and left home.

At work, she decided to have a tea with her toast she ordered. It was one of those boring days because she had to prepare summaries of many project suggestions.

Galina has opened the safe, took pictures of the documents and delivered them to Mariya without any problem and she decided to celebrate her problem-free and successful mission with home-made vareniki (a kind of pastry filled with potatoes or more often with sour cherries). There was another celebration to which she was not invited. But Galina was not aware of it. After getting close with John, she was under surveillance of MIT for 24 hours a day. John was a high-level executive and had high level contacts and relationships. This was enough to be on his tail, too.

As soon as the control that Galina was performing with a detector was noticed thanks to the cameras that had been planted in John's house and that were able to record every angle, the one in his bedroom was withdrawn. In order not to be detected, the camera was withdrawn to the ultimate point in the camera hole which was several meters of length back in the wall. It was determined that Galina was searching the house to find something; when the camera got back to its position, it recorded Galina while she was opening the case and photographing the documents.

Furthermore, they have found the microchip placed between the bristles of toilet brush with a device sensitive to electronic signals, copied it and put it back. The marks Galina left at the house were still intact when she left just like she had entered the house.

Galina was fulfilling all demands of SVR, observing everybody at UN-HCR and acting indifferent and naive. She was trying to obtain information regarding personal data of employees, their subjects of work, the budget of UN for each project and all other subjects.

The team working on Galina decided to engage Galina. Galina was not a service employee with power to access classified information, but she may have this power in future. But they were aware that it would not be this easy. It was necessary to understand what would prod someone into action as Machiavelli dwelled upon. Was it love? Money? Power?

What was it?

In this context, it could be said that not being assigned illegally, that is not as a diplomat made her resent SVR and her country. However, this alone was not enough for engagement. They should find more.

Her doctorate friends were not aware of Galina's weaknesses, they were not spending time together and sharing nothing. Galina wasn't talking about herself. She was a good listener!

Two doctorate students were chosen to approach to make Galina develop her relationships with her friends in doctorate class. One of them was Pelin and the other was Osman.

But when families of Pelin and Osman are investigated, it was decided not to use them.

Time was flying and they were running out of time. Russians were unpredictable, so Galina would be called back to head office and assigned at somewhere else, regardless of her successful works in Turkey. They should decide and fast. A brilliant idea has occurred to Teoman.

Galina was having lunch every day with her coworkers at a nearby restaurant.

One day Galina talked with three of her friends regarding where to go for lunch. Would it be the restaurant serving home meals on the street or the other one serving toasts and appetizers? As a matter of fact, their favorite restaurant was the one right across their office. But they were there yesterday, and they decided to go the restaurant serving home meals.

They sat at the last empty table. The waiter brought the menus and recommended sauce meatballs. Instead of sauce meatballs suggested by the waiter, Galina ordered chicken drumstick. Galina has been warned not to eat the meals recommended to her. Her friends ordered sauce meatballs.

They have moved into deep conversation while they ate, and they noticed that the lunch-break was about to end. They immediately left the restaurant.

Galina sat at her desk and got ready to prepare the final reports. Because they should be submitted today. She was working at the last report after two hours had passed and she had a stomachache. She ran to toilet and couldn't stand up from the toilet bowl. Her blood pressure dropped.

She murmured, "Bladskaya kuritsa-bitch chicken!"

It was chicken poisoning. She recovered herself, called Livinia in the next room and asked her to take her to a hospital. Liviana called a cab and they immediately went to a nearby private hospital. They admitted to emergency service. Galina was turned pale. She put herself on the stretcher.

When Galina regained consciousness, she felt a pain in her throat. They irrigated her stomach. She closed her eyes and fell into sleep.

When she opened her eyes, she noticed that she was being drip-fed and there was another patient next to her. She closed his eyes again and tried to have a rest. Her stomach was upside down. It was very hard to bear. She heard that chicken poisoning was bad, but she didn't think it was this bad. It was a very bad experience.

She opened her eyes again and looked around to see if the other patient was still there. That patient was also drip-fed. A little while later Livinia came, touched her face and caressed her hair. Galina opened her eyes and Lavinia asked how she felt. "Not too bed," said Galina. Liviana said, "I have talked with your doctor. He said you should stay here tonight." Galina replied, "It doesn't matter."

Next morning a nurse visited her and said, "I hope you'll get well soon." Galina thanked her. She measured her blood pressure and checked the serum. Then she measured the blood pressure of other patient, checked his serum and said, "Get well soon." Then a doctor came and wrote something on the paper at the foot of the bed. After filling the papers of other patient, the doctor said food poisoning is very common these days and she should be very careful when she eats outside. Then he left the room.

Meanwhile, a young and beautiful woman came to visit the other patient. She brought him flowers. She kissed him and said, "Get well soon darling." She asked him how he was feeling. "Not bad," said the man. "I think you need to eat homemade meals," said the woman. The man nodded. "I am late for work," said the woman, "they will discharge you soon. Go home and have some rest. She kissed his cheek and left. The woman said, "Get well" to Galina and Galina thanked her.

Galina realized that the man was also there because of food-poisoning and asked him so. "Unfortunately" said the man wearily.

"I didn't know food-poisoning was this bad," said Galina. Mine was chicken-poisoning. Yours?" The man sad "Me, too," and continued, "Where are you from? "Russia" said Galina.

The man asked again, "How long you've been in Turkey? Your Turkish is very fluent."

"It's been only 6 months, but I have studied Turkish in Russia."

"Really? How nice! Do you work in Ankara?"

"I work at UNHCR. What's your occupation?"

"I work at the Ministry of National Defense."

When she heard that the man works at the Ministry of National Defense Galina felt a glow of happiness. She has found the source candidate she was looking for. The man looked a bit naive. She would accomplish a result if she plays her cards right.

"Your work must be enjoyable," said Galina.

"No," said the man, "tiresome and stressful."

Before leaving the room, Galina said, "I hope you get well soon." Galina headed towards the corridor and when she was in front of the lift, she put her hand on the wall and acted as is feels dizzy. Her roommate was right after her. "Do you feel dizzy?" asked the man. Galina said, "Yes." They got on the lift together.

"I forgot to ask your name," said Galina. "Doruk Yilmaz."

"And I am Galina Ivanova."

At the same time, they said, "Glad to meet you."

Galina looked into his eyes. "I still don't know where to find some of my needs in Turkey and it seems I will never find out as I am so busy. Maybe you can give me your phone number and I can call you if I need something?" There was a spark in his eyes. "Sure, why not?"

*

Galina gave all contact information of the man she plans to use as an information source to Mariya for confirmation and the information that Mariya gave her during another gym session was far and away the best. The man was in charge of supervising high-tech heavy weaponry projects within the Ministry of National Defense. He was supervising numerous projects and preparing presentations for the approval of the commission. She knew the importance of such presentations. There might be some high-risk projects which the commission would not approve and if she can make him present these projects in the last minute, the commission would approve them without discussing in detail and consequently heavy weapons of Turks would not operate properly.

Galina looked at Mariya. "Did you ask them the matter I told you? What did they say?" Mariya ignored her question.

"Do you see your mother? How is she?"

"She's OK. John uses me like an animal. What did they say? You told them I was dripping wet, right?"

"Of course."

"They didn't accept it, right?"

"Unfortunately, not."

"Tell them again. I cannot go on like this. There are some things which I cannot do even for my country."

"Please! They might get rough, you know."

"What did they tell you?"

"You don't want to hear."

"Mariya! Just say it."

"It is better to get wet while you are free than shriveling in a dungeon."

Galina was so angry. Her hands were shaking. A thought passed through her mind. "Insolent Russians. There is no humanity in them."

"If you seek for something where it doesn't exist, then you are not seeking for it"

Rumi

"Please calm down," said Mariya. "Let's talk about your prospect? What should be the plan to talk to him?"

It was impossible to wait in front of the Ministry of National Defense to arrange a coincidental meeting. Waiting there would attract attention and she would get caught. She decided not to take any risk and try a less risky method.

She called Doruk the next day at lunch break and asked him how he feels with a fluent Turkish. Then she told him that the heating boiler at her home was suddenly stopped working. The service personnel have told her that the boiler was very old, and it should be replaced. So, they will get her boiler for maintenance and would it be possible for him to help her. She also told him that the landlord will deduct the price of the boiler from the rental. She did not forget to call the boiler service the day before and call the landlord after the service personnel left.

Galina and Doruk decided to meet in front of the Atatürk statue in Ulus at 1:00 pm on Saturday. Doruk told her they will go to Ruzgarli Street.

In the evening, Galina went to the cafe where she and her friends play dart. They were making a dart tournament, but her underperformance was surprising for her friends. Galina was thinking about what she will do the next day when she meets with Doruk and couldn't play well. Liviana had to score abullseye " at her last throw.

She threw the dart and leaped, "At last!"

Galina was never this happy for the game to end. Jade, a co-worker smiled at Galina, "You are so exhausted as if you have conducted the mission of UN today."

The next morning, Galina stared at the mirror. Turkey was a neighboring country. The weapons produced in Turkey and controlled by Doruk would be used against her country one day. She needed to prepare Doruk for the task and there was no room for error.

When Galina arrived there, Doruk was waiting for her in front of the statue. They shook hands. Galina has made Doruk wait for almost ten minutes. She didn't need to coddle Doruk. In fact, Doruk should be the one to coddle her. So, she would act normal.

On their way to Ruzgarli Street, they have talked about so many things and Doruk's talkativeness didn't bore her. Galina just kept listening to him. She was making Doruk speak. Doruk has told her so many things from his university years to his first employment as a civil servant. Galina didn't want to arouse suspicion with her questions. Doruk kept talking.

Boilers were really nice but expensive. Galina chose one of the cheapest models. She noted the model and brand asked if there will be any markdown.

"I will do my best," said the seller, "make up your mind and the rest is easy."

"You also make up your mind" said Galina. Doruk interrupted, "My friend will consider your offer and we'll be back."

"When you make up your mind, we'll go together to buy the boiler. It doesn't seem easy for you to deal with these people. He didn't want to offense you."

"Okay."

"I'll take a cab to Kizilay. I can leave you there if you want."

"Sure."

They took the first can they found on the main street. Traffic was heavy but cab driver knew how to drive, and they arrived to Kizilay in a short time.

"I will go to the shared-cab station," said Galina, You can drop me somewhere around here."

"I'll go that way too."

"I think we can buy the boiler next week."

"I hope the boiler can stand one more week."

"Shall we meet at the same place and time next Saturday?"

"Okay! I something comes up, we'll be in touch."

Galina was walking to shared-taxi station and thinking, "If nothing happens, we should make a phone call. Doruk's phone might be wire trapped."

The week passed very fast. It was another classic Friday night. This time she performed very good because she knew exactly what to do with Doruk and her friends were so surprised again. Because she was playing so well as if she was in a professional tournament.

Galina came back home at 11:00 pm. Doruk has not called Galina. Galina was sure that Doruk will be in Ulus tomorrow.

When she woke up the next morning, she felt fresh. Because she had a sound sleep. It was like beauty sleep.

Galina checked her high-heels if their heels were dry. They were dry. It was a simple trick and scenario was ready. She has planned to break the heel on purpose when they leave the boiler shop.

Galina was late for 10 minutes again. She was wearing black pants showing her body lines and a skin-color blouse showing her bra.

Doruk looked at Galina and thought what a slim waist she has.

They started walking towards Ruzgarli Street. Doruk was talking and talking. Doruk has bargained with the seller and Galina paid the money. They were to call Galina to tell her the date and time of the service personnel will come to install the boiler.

Galina broke her heel as she planned and held Doruk's arm. Doruk was surprised.

"Oy boje (My God)," said Galina.

Doruk told her to hold her. Galina took Doruk's arm and they walked towards the cab station. "I can take you home with pleasure," Doruk said and smiled.

When they arrived at Galina's building,

Doruk asked if there is an elevator in the building.

"Yes, we have but it keeps stopping. Once I stuck in it and I don't use it since then."

"Then let me come with you."

"Then let me offer you a cup of coffee!"

Doruk got out of the cab and helped Galina. Galina smiled.

Doruk was so happy because their plan was working so well. Doruk recalled how they detected the restaurants Galina favors, placing their agents in the kitchens of all restaurants the same day and the argument they had with the owner of a restaurant, who didn't let them place a man in his kitchen even after he saw their MIT IDs.

He thought about the wheat-colored dust showing the effect of food-poisoning, the cab which has taken Galina to hospital. That cab was one of theirs. He also recalled his colleague who played the role of his girlfriend at the hospital.

Galina opened the door and handed slippers to Doruk. Doruk has preferred his fake name to be Doruk Yilmaz, who was really an official in the Ministry because he thought that the internal phone directory of the Ministry would have been seized. So Teoman would play the role of real Doruk Yilmaz. Doruk went to the living room and sat down. Galina asked him if he would like to have cognac or liqueur. Doruk asked for cognac.

Galina put some aphrodisiac both in his coffee and cognac. She had to put three drops. But it was difficult, so she hit the bottle with her index finger, but eight drops went into the cognac.

"This sheep may go out now and call out is there anybody to fuck me," thought Galina.

Galina and Doruk have conversed for 35 minutes without interruption. During the first 15 minutes, Doruk's face turned red. When she holds Galina's arm and touched her breasts, he had this feeling even if it was at low level. In order to play the role of real Doruk Yilmaz, Doruk has memorized many weaponry projects of the past, engineering terms, courses at the university...very well even if sexual urge has been increased.

Galina was beating around the bush and she managed to tell him how they have played "spin the bottle" when she was at middle school and her first kissing experiences. As she talked, she never took her eyes away from Doruk.

"Eyes looking at directly show shamelessness and winking eyes show indecisiveness."

Aristotle

Under the influence of the drug and alcohol she asked, "Should the bottle be empty to play this game?"

Galina said, "If the woman is ready, then there is no need."

She sat on Doruk's lap and began kissing him. In the bedroom Doruk was thinking, "I never thought having sex would be a part of my job."

When Doruk regained consciousness, Galina was cooking in the kitchen. Doruk got out of bed. He put his pants on and went to the kitchen.

"I am cooking for you," said Galina.

They ate their meal and it was already 9:00 pm.

Doruk said, "I should go. I am working at the Ministry of National Defense and if I talk you on the phone, it would be a problem. So, I will buy a line on the name of a friend and let you know."

"Whatever you want."

"I will also buy a new phone and bring it to you tomorrow night around 8:00 pm. Okay?"

"Okay."

"That is, if you want."

"What do you think?" she said and kissed him.

Two Months Later

Doruk has found out all weaknesses of Galina: Her mother, nymphomania, wearing style attire, love for her country and hatred she felt in her subconscious.

Galina once said, "Russia is the country of injustice."

Doruk though, "As if America is any different!"

But he knew that the most significant weakness or desire of Galina was having a child. Whenever they watch a movie together, Galina's eyes were filling with tears when there is a scene showing a mother and child. It seemed Galina really wanted to have a child.

Galina too had learned Doruk's weaknesses. In her biographical intelligence report to SVR about Doruk she stated that Doruk was keen on money, comfort, dressing up smartly, spending lots of money and entertainment. He also had the belief that his position should be higher, and he was resenting the ministry and the state because he was not promoted as he deserves.

SVR has sent a message to Galina to use money to convince Doruk.

And Galina begun getting some petty gifts for Doruk. By giving the petty gifts, Galina was getting some answers. The answers were being forwarded to head office by Mariya for confirmation. Questions were simple so confirmation was not taking much time. Doruk was accepting all her gifts such as ties, wristlets, watches without hesitation.

Doruk planned. He was going to tell Galina that he needs money and borrow some from her. This would make Galina to believe that he was addicted to Galina. This should not be as complicated as previous plans. It should be plain and simple. But there would be no need for that.

One evening Doruk and Galina were having dinner at her home. Galina talked about the mission of UN in Turkey and all around the world. Then she made an offer to Doruk. Doruk would inform her about the projects in return of 3,000 dollars per month. She also told him that he would get more money depending on the information he'll provide. Doruk looked at her and ask, "What is with you, Galina? What do you want?" Galina told him that she was working in UN's disarmament programme and collecting information and her aim was preventing the weapons produced in NATO countries to fall into the hands of terrorists. They also wanted to detect the producers of the confiscated weapons and they were completely working for the sake of world peace.

Doruk nodded as is he believed her. "You are right! It is possible for the projects developed in our country to be stolen or the weapons produced here may fall into the hands of terrorists. I don't think we have a strong data security system, either." But he needed to think about her offer.

Galina looked at him and said, "And we won't need to be discreet about our relationship anymore. If you want, we can invite your girlfriend and the presenter who keeps stalking me, even though he is a student in Bilkent University and hang on together?"

"Might be but Ela is angry with me because I've been neglecting her lately. I have to win her heart again."

Galina has arranged a nice environment to mask both her source and activities. She felt she managed very well.

Doruk was happy to play a love game with Galina but it became very hard for him to endure the pressure of his manager to engage Galina urgently.

Doruk was providing insignificant real info and untrue information which create the impression as if they are important. He gave Galina a map showing the locations of ground-to-air and ground-to-ground missile systems and long-range missile batteries buried in Erzurum. There were real missiles at the locations spotted on the map.

It was a historical fact that respected persons who were imams in the region during Ottoman-Russian War were actually Russians even though they spoke Turkish fluently and they have made sabotages during the war. There might be sleeper Russian agents in Turkey. There was no doubt that they would check the targets on the map.

Turks have decided to deploy the long-range missile systems recently developed at home, so they didn't mind providing the information regarding their old locations.

Deception has been a mutual game throughout the history.

Doruk also didn't want to ruin the game of love they play. Because he liked spending time with Galina. Who wouldn't like spending time with her? On the other hand, he wanted to align Galina with Turks and obtain information from her. But Galina didn't seem to be ready to change sides yet.

Doruk requested his friends to follow them when he meets with Galina to find out if they were being followed by SVR. He was asking for counter-follow up and his director got suspicious of him. Once his director looked at him over his glasses when he was examining a document and asked, "Do you want this to feel okay or because you think of the girl?"

In response Doruk said, "I only want to know if SVR has suspicions about Galina, that's all."

His director has asked him, "If they are suspicious, then what?"

When Doruk offered to provide more serious information and documents to Galina, his director said, "We'll see."

After leaving his room, Ahmet went to see the director. He was Doruk's co-worker. Ahmet was jealous of Doruk's success. The directors at MIT were so smart and deliberate. It was impossible to deceive them. So, has planned to increase the pressure on Doruk indirectly.

Ahmet wanted Doruk to be disenchanted with the directors. He wanted to deal major blows to Doruk and cause him to make mistakes. His father was a close friend of the director and using this he changed the subject.

"With all due respect, I have to tell you something Sir. Doruk is very absent-minded lately. I hope he doesn't have a problem. Do you know anything about it?"

"As far as I am concerned, he has no problems."

Ahmet had chosen his words so meticulously. A thought has passed through the director's mind, "Would Doruk be in love with the Russian?"

Doruk was called to his director's office on Monday morning. It seemed that everybody was so busy. Doruk was about to tell his mission, his phone rang and Doruk went out. When he entered the office again, a written note was given to his director. The director was rushing from his office to meeting room. Doruk was tired of waiting.

His director stormed in. He looked at Doruk. Sat in his chair. "Finish the job! Do whatever you do but finish it! Do you get it?" he yelled. He was so angry and wreaked his anger on Doruk.

"Okay Sir," said Doruk. His face was chalk white when he came out.

He was in the corridor of his department and he was having difficulty to walk. His friends who knew that Doruk was working on Galina said, "Since the boss made him wait this long, there must be something important." Ahmet didn't want to be involved so he said, "He granted Doruk the power of making expenses." Yavuz recalled that the director asked them to monitor Doruk and Galina last Saturday and perform audio surveillance. So, he knew that there was something wrong and didn't make any comment.

Their director was so smart not to assign this mission to Ahmet. Because he believed that the matters should be assessed by different minds.

Doruk went out alone for lunch. "Why the boss is this obsessed with this woman? He spends time and effort and also makes me do the same thing. I don't understand. What if we directly offer money?"

He ate his lunch and got back to work.

"I will meet with Galina tonight, have some pleasure and the rest will take care of itself," he thought. He had a nice dinner and pleasurable night with Galina.

He woke up early in the morning. He hopped in the shower. He was suffocated and he couldn't have full ablution because his mind was so busy. He intended but then forgot all about it and did it again. Then he forgot how many times he had gargled and gargled again. He got out of the shower after 45 minutes. He was confused.

Doruk was so tired in the shower that when he sat down at breakfast his forehead was sweating.

When they were having breakfast, Galina asked why the shower took so long Doruk ignored her question. While he was thinking that offering money to Galina would have an adverse result, Galina said, "You are so absent-minded. You didn't drink too much last night. What's wrong, is there a problem?" "I had a nightmare last night and trying to remember it," said Doruk.

After leaving Galina's house, Doruk decided to stroll around Eymir Lake and went back home to change.

Doruk didn't think that Eymir would be this crowded in the morning. When he approached the first of the kiosks near the lake, he decided to buy tea. He got his tea and sat on a stool. He watched the lake. Two women were chatting next to him. Doruk began to listen to these women. One of them said, "It is really unbelievable. How many times did Nazan have a miscarriage? After the last one of her relatives told her that there is a society in Adana and if she goes there and ask the hodja to pray for her and keep the prayer of the hodja on her, she would not have a miscarriage. Many women gave birth this way. When Nazan knew that she was pregnant again, she and her husband went to Adana. Hodja prayed for Nazan and touched her face with his hand." The other woman asked, "What is a society?" The other woman replied, "Some kind of a shrine."

"Very interesting," thought Doruk. Everything depends on prayer." Then he wondered. If he impregnates Galina, would she share everything she know with him? "I will impregnate her and then I'll ensure she will have a miscarriage" And I will tell her my real identity. I will tell her that I am really in love with her. It may work." Then something else hit him, "What if she doesn't suffer a miscarriage?" He then shouted, "God damn t!"

He was still so confused when he arrived at the office. He should plan. He had to make Galina to provide information to him.

He had to raise the wall of lies between him and Galina, but in doing so he should not be the father of a Russian agent's child. They should be sincere. But how?

He has thought for hours. He went home. He continued to think in silence without turning on the TV. Finally, he said, "I've got it!" He was going to remove the wall of lies with another lie. He would find and use a neutering medicine, tell Galina that he is in love with her, he wants to make a child with her and try to impregnate her. For a moment, he reproached himself for thinking to use a sacred emotion like motherhood. Then he recovered himself. It was his duty. Duty always comes first. Sacredness was belong to the star and crescent flag. He should tell his idea to the director. He grabbed the phone and called him. "I want to see if you're available, it is important," he said. "I am in," said the director, "come here!" "I'm at home! You will not go out in half an hour, will you?" "I will be here."

When he went there, the director said, "Shoot!" "What's so important?" he asked. Doruk told his plan. "It's a wonderful plan. Find a good doctor and talk. I don't want any problem, okay?"

Doruk prayed for the injection to work. When they were having dinner, her mother Elif asked, "Do you have a problem my son?" "I have difficult job mom, I need to finish it," said Doruk. "My son can handle it" said Elif and held his hand.

Doruk was going over his plan during dinner. Their dinner was this silent for the first time. Doruk's father was martyred by terrorist organization called PKK in Kiziltepe, Mardin and since then, Elif has been spending her time with Doruk and their conversations was always very long.

Captain Riza, Doruk's father has been martyred when a MIT agent infiltrated into PKK was demasked and executed. When the MIT agent was demasked and before MIT was informed about his execution and without waiting for the period to understand why the information flow was stopped, PKK has attacked and Captain Riza was martyred. The state was not informed about the attack and it was an intelligence weakness. So Doruk knew that intelligence is so important and decided to be an intelligence officer so that other children would not grow without their fathers.

Looking at Doruk's face, Elif thought, "Just like his father!" When Doruk was out of the nursery with her mother in his childhood, he always looked at the migrating birds and said, "Hey birds, tell my father that mom and I have missed him so much." Elif has never forgotten this. Because a few hours later, they received the bad news. Doruk would have understood that her father was martyred.

Whenever he spends time with Galina, Doruk was touching her as is he feels her in her heart and holding her hand while they sleep on the bed. He was sensually kissing Galina on her lips and embracing her. Galina has felt this change. Doruk's feelings were enough to affect Galina. Galina always felt worthless in her relations in Russia and Crimea. She felt she was valued for the first time in her life.

Doruk was predicting all risks beforehand. He had neutering injections for six months and every time, he waited for three days to see Galina because he wanted the mark of the injection to go away. Doruk made his decision. He bought a bucket of yellow roses before going to Galina's house. The bucket had seven roses because even-numbered flowers meant bad luck for Russians.

Doruk became a standing joke at the office after the injection. Limited number of his friends who were aware of the operation have been laying eyes on Doruk. "I want to tell you something?" said Murat.

Doruk replied, "Okay but nothing indirect or secret" "If you need support, just tell me," said Murat and laughed.

When Galina opened the door, she grabbed the flowers and smelled them. "Thank you very much, Doruk." She filled the vase with water and placed the flowers in it.

Doruk has been in love with Galina for the last two months but he developed some behavioral patterns as he didn't want her to know this. Whenever he is at her home, he was asking some trivial questions like "What did you do today? Where did you eat with your friends? There were no men, right?" As

Doruk was not telling his feelings to her, Galina kept thinking, "This must be Turkish style love."

One day Doruk said,

"Now we know each other well. We don't need to be protected during sex. "

"I agree. But let's be careful so I won't get pregnant. I can't trust hospitals in Turkey for abortion."

"When I look at you, I believe that you would have beautiful child."

"This is a sensitive subject Doruk, let's drop it."

"I am 40 years old. If I get pregnant, I won't consider abortion."

"So what? Should I have a child?"

"Actually, I have never given a thought to it and I don't plan to have a child but if it is from you, I won't be unhappy."

Galina's eyes were filled with tears. She hugged Doruk and started to cry.

"The key to deception is doing just the opposite of what's expected from you. That is appearing weak when you are strong, passive when you are active, close when you are away and away when you are close"

Sun Tzu

Doruk slept all night cuddling Galina. This has aroused a different feeling. He felt a slight ache but when he cuddled her, he felt as if there is a green substance in his stomach. Was it love? When Doruk got up in the morning, Galina was already up and prepared breakfast.

After the breakfast, Doruk held her hand and took her to bedroom by saying, "I have a surprise for you." He undressed Galina and they made love.

When Galina knew that Doruk was about to ejaculate, she tried to get up but Doruk didn't let her. Galina was shocked. She hugged Doruk and kissed him with a smile in her eyes. She put her head on his shoulder for a while. Then she got up and lied on the bed. She kept her legs closed. Galina's eyes were closed but she looked so happy and it was worth to see. Doruk knew he did a great job. Now it was time to convince Galina to change sides before pregnancy and child. This was even harder.

Galina asked Doruk to buy a pregnancy test device from the pharmacy and he did. The result was negative. Galina was demoralized. "Sometimes women get pregnant after the first intercourse and sometimes after the tenth," said Doruk. Galina was hopeful.

Galina felt she was valued for the first time. She has learned what value is from Doruk and she also felt that she has never valued anyone till today. Doruk would be the first person she cares for.

*

Doruk gave a document to Galina once a month, and he even though had the second injection, he acted as if he wanted to impregnate her.

When their relationship was made regular, Doruk started to apply the second phase of his plan. He didn't come home on Wednesday evening to meet Galina. Galina couldn't reach him by phone.

"He must have run out of battery," she thought.

An hour has passed. She called him again. His phone was still off. Galina begun to worry. What if they understood that Doruk was giving information to her? Or did they uncover the operation? There was some abnormality but what. It happened for the first time.

Doruk decided not to prolong his plan. He knew that if Galina cannot reach him for an unreasonably long time, she would notify SVR and maybe she would be called back by SVR. Therefore, Doruk was not to sleep till 5:00 am and sweat by running on the treadmill in his suit. Thus, he would go to Galina's house at 5:30 am in sweat as if he was interrogated for hours.

Doruk went to Galina's house around 5:30 am. He rang the doorbell. When she heard the doorbell, Galina jumped out of her bed. She pressed the button of the intercom and asked, "Who is this?"

"It's me," said Doruk.

When he was out of the lift, Doruk was looking so weak. "What happened Doruk?" asked Galina.

Doruk went in and begun telling, "One of the relatives of a parliament member has gun factory. I gave him drawings of a few models we have developed. There were undercover cops at the restaurant. Stupid bastard has put some money in an envelope. I handed the flash disk and he suddenly took out a yellow envelop and gave it to me. First, I took the envelop but I returned it immediately. Undercover cops were for something else, but they called another team and they

50

took us into custody. We have been at the police station since 7:30 pm last night."

"What will happen now?" asked Galina excitedly.

"Nothing! I don't know. While we were there, a civilian dressed man came. He said you are a Russian agent and told me about your activities here."

Galina's eyes were almost popping out of her head when she heard this. Galina was about to ask if they have mentioned Mariya and John, but she didn't.

Doruk told his conversation with the man.

"Did Galina ask for information, documents, etc. from you?"

"No! I've just heard she is a spy now."

" Shut up! I am not stupid! We know what you have received and what you have given. If you don't want to go to prison, tell Galina to work with us or you will both go jail and stay there for the rest of your lives."

"I'll talk to her."

"You'd better do!"

Then he looked at Galina's eyes. "Yes Miss Galina. I am in love with you. I even think of having a child with you, but you hide your real identity from me. If you have not tricked me by saying that you were working at UN's disarmament programme, I wouldn't give you those documents. You have treated me like a fool. We'll go to hospital tomorrow and if you are pregnant, we'll have the child aborted."

Galina abruptly started crying. She ran to the bedroom immediately. Doruk opened the fridge door to play the role of an angry and deceived man. There was only Martini Bianco in the fridge. He took the bottle and went to the bedroom as he downed the half bottle. He laid down just next to Galina without taking off his suit. But he did not hold her hand nor did he hug her.

Doruk recalled Mr. Burak who had taught him much when he first started working. While he was laying down, he suddenly thought, "I guess I have passed the apprenticeship and, on my way, to become a master. Though I do not think that I will ever be a conspirator just as he used to be." Then he recalled the report which Mr. Burak had taken from the psychologist and read to him. Then he remembered the statements in the report, "Galina's sense of worthlessness will result in glorifying you in her eyes. Since her feeling of inadequacy will spring after glorifying you, she will start to nurture enmity towards you unconsciously; eventually, the moment she senses a shadow of the inadequacy of you, the enmity in her subconscious will reach the surface of her mind.

In addition, those who have an attitude in which they accept their self-worthlessness may despise you whenever they have found the slightest deficit of yours, thinking that they will be valued only by a worthless person."

He had to play his part well, in this context. Just as his manager told him, he had to tell her "I love you" not very often. If he increased the frequency of that, the question "Why does he always state this?" might arise in her mind. He had to never forget that Galina was a member of SVR.

Galiba kept crying. In order not to disrupt his ordinary behavior and to prove that he still loved her, he hugged her; however, he removed his arm from Galina's shoulder and turned his back. In ordinary conditions, Doruk had to react to the fact that Galina made a fool of him and caused him trouble.

It was 10:00 in the morning when Doruk woke up. He turned his head and looked at Galina. Galina was still sleeping. Galiba had suffered serious trauma. He thought to himself that she would not get up easily. Galina's phone rang. Galina was able to open only one eye. Her other eye had become gummy since she had cried laying on her side and the tears from her open eye had flowed onto her other eye.

She picked up the phone. "Hello," she said. "I got sick last night, I don't think I am able to come to work. Would you inform me?" Galina asked.

Doruk got out of bed. He washed his face. Then, he went to the living room and turned on the TV. He crossed his feet on the side table. He started changing channels. After a while, he heard that Galina got up from the bed. She was probably washing her face in the bathroom. She came to the living room where Doruk was.

"I'm so sorry, Doruk. I wouldn't want that to happen in this way."

"What are you sorry for? For the guys who had learned everything about you?" Or for that, I found out that you were making a fool out of me?

"For deceiving you."

"Doruk, you have given me the most value until this day, you have made me feel my womanhood, you asked me to have a child with me, you are a sun that has risen in my life. You mean more than anyone and anything to me."

Doruk remained silent and did not react to her words. "Do you understand?" Galina asked. Doruk was still not saying a word. Galina sat down next to Doruk. Her tears flowed as if they had been a stream.

Doruk wiped Galina's tears from her cheeks. "Please, don't cry anymore. What is done, is done," he said.

Galina went to the kitchen and brewed her a cup of coffee, saying "I need to have a coffee to pull myself together." And she made some breakfast for Doruk.

Doruk was such a workaholic that he was going through his plan in his mind as Galina kept apologizing and looking at him imploringly.

"Galina, maybe what is done is the best for us,"

"Yes... What is happening is happening for something good."

"If it weren't for you, there would be nothing for me to convince you. They would put me in jail right off the bat. Maybe they would put you in jail too unless there was a chance to reach me through you."

"Yep."

"Galina, let's do what they have asked, for us. I'll be free and you'll be free. Then we will be able to continue our relationship wherever we have left it."

"But tell them that I need to keep sending the information and the documents which I have taken from you to the headquarters."

"Okay, I'll tell them that, but they will definitely change my place afterward or they will never assign me any projects and will never allow me to join the meetings. I do not know what they are going to do. In this case, I can only provide whatever they give me, do not except something original as before. The guy will come to my workplace on Monday. I will tell him that you are ready to cooperate, then."

Galina found herself thinking what her child would look like if he or she was from Doruk. She did not answer the question.

"I'll say okay?" Doruk asked.

Squinting her eyes, Galina nodded and continued, saying "Tell them that I am not doing this for money, I'm doing this for you."

"I'll them," Doruk said.

"The one who loves less directs the relationship. Because the one who loves the most says okay to everything, because of the fear of losing."

Erich Fromm

They talked about Galina's secret world all day, laying on the bed. She had had so many disappointments in her life. She was thinking that no one pays attention to her. She was believing that only her mother loved her. Everyone had used her. She was thinking that even her mother had used her at some point. "How so?" Doruk asked. "My mother got pregnant against her will so that my father wouldn't leave her. My father always used to tell that when he was drunk. Therefore, he never loved me, he sold the piano to get even with me. I never played the piano again," she said.

Galina told him that she hadn't found what she had been expecting from SVR. Then she continued her words, "They sent me here without immunity instead of appointing me as an embassy employee. Of course, if my father or mother would be a high-ranking officer somewhere, they would have not done that and would have sent me to best places, assigned the best diplomatic missions to me with diplomatic immunity, and would have tried to win the favor of my mother and father."

"It is a predisposition of human nature to consider an unpleasant idea untrue, and then it is easy to find arguments against it."

Sigmund Freud

Doruk realized that when Galina was talking about her family, she never used the word "family" and she used only "my mother" and "my father." Galina was really a white pigeon with a broken wing. As a matter of fact, he felt quite sorry for Galina. But there was no room to feel sorry in Doruk's business. Doruk was fighting a battle, so to say. However, the quality and the extent of the war had changed. It was a secret war with no name. His nerves had to be as strong as steel and his emotions had to be blinded.

Doruk was fighting his own feelings. Whenever Galina crossed his mind, he evoked his father immediately. Even so, Galina was in his mind when he is laying down. And the first thing to cross his mind in the morning when he woke up was also Galina. It was as if he devoted his soul to her as if Galina was living inside of Doruk. But Doruk could not face his feelings and was unable to bring himself to the thought that he was in love with her. He kept the fact that USA, EU, Iran, Iraq, and Syria, as well as Russia, supported the terror organization PKK.

He had established his life on that fact. The only Russian person Doruk was in contact with was Galina. Therefore, when they drunk with Galina, he was trying to keep a cool head and not to spill out his hated against her. When the fact that the neutering injection was possible to leave him infertile forever came to his mind, the urge to avenge his father outweighed, and his sense of mission was above all.

"When evaluating a person, it is quite beneficial to know that where he could push the hatred which bedights people with a personal and characteristic trait."

Alfred Adler

When Doruk came to Galina's place on Monday evening, he told her that he had talked to the guy and that the guy had said, "Nothing is going to happen to Galina or you as long as Galina keeps working for us."

"When your time is here over, go to Russia and submit your resignation, and after that let's marry here," Doruk told Galina.

Galina was so happy when she heard the word "marry" but she told Doruk, "If I resign, I will not be able to get out of Russia for a period that they determine, and I find a way to get out, they will definitely find me and kill me. The leaving ban may change depending on the situation, but it is at least five years."

"What if I come to Russia, can you find a job there?"

"I can but since you will have no information to give to me, they will not allow me to see you. If our meeting is detected, they will either put me in jail or kill me."

"Alright... Then how are we supposed to keep in contact?"

"I am here, and I am going nowhere for a while. When I am called to the headquarters and my workplace is changed, then we will discuss it. Now let's enjoy our togetherness and not think about the future."

Before this crucial conversation, Doruk's manager had told him, "Do not utter a word that would make it impossible for you to leave the country, such as departure ban. Because we need to keep the emotional bond between you warm, and in order to maintain this task, you need to ply between Turkey and wherever Galina is appointed after Turkey."

While he was considering the manager had told him, he pointed the sofa and said, "I'll lay down here a while, I feel so tired. Stress ruined me." He dropped the subject.

The more he talked, the higher the risk. Galina thought about laying a blanket on Doruk at first, but she woke him up and sent him to bed.

Doruk got out of the bed, puffing as if depressed in the morning. Galina said, "Good morning," when he was getting up from the bed. Doruk pretended not to have heard that and went into the bathroom. After washing his face, he started to look at the mirror at length. Because he wanted Galina to see him looking at her when she woke up. Because that was what depressed people were doing in the movies.

Doruk went to the living room and turned on the TV, like always. Instead of calling out to Galina lovingly, "Love, come on, wake up!" he called out to her stonily, "Galina, wake up."

Galina came to Doruk and complained, "Won't you ever call me love anymore?"

"I will but give me some time. Don't push me, you see how stressed I am, right?" asked Doruk.

Doruk finished his breakfast, demonstrating an Oscar-nominated performance even though he hadn't received any acting training, he put on his shoes and kissed Galina on the cheek unwillingly and downheartedly.

Doruk started to behave as if he had bounced back on the following days. He started asking questions such as her SVR training and training place without pushing too hard and as if he was actually asking them and started to write the answers on his notebook. Galina asked from an intelligence perspective,

"What is the thing with the notebook?"

"I think it's an ordinary one."

"Some notebooks have hard but thin papers so that what you are writing cannot be read on the other pages."

His manages was investigating their conversations daily, evaluating them, and trying to analyze whether Doruk became the prey as he was the hunter. Doruk was conveying all the details about their conversations and meeting. His manager knew that Doruk was a son of a martyr, but trust was not an obstacle to check.

Galina realized that her head was aching when she opened her eyes in the morning. She needed to stay in the bed for a while. When she looked at the clock, she rolled out of the bed slowly, thinking that she was going to get ready for a picture gallery. When she was taking a shower, she determined that her headache was due to whether SVR would find out that she sided with Turkey. She was so tired both physically and mentally that she decided to reward herself with going to SPA in Hilton Hotel.

She wore her blue blouse with shoulder cleavage and her long skirt, which were suiting her well. She glanced at the mirror. She one more realized her beauty. Then, suddenly her phone rang. She looked for his phone in her room, check under her pajamas, and then she realized that the sound came from the bathroom. She still could not come to life, that was why she was not able to perceive where the sound was coming from.

When she went to the bathroom and picked up her phone, she saw that Mariya was calling her all along. She answered the phone.

"Hello."

"Hi, Gala."

"Hi, Masha."

"What are you doing?"

"There's a gallery and I'm getting ready for it."

"I feel a little bit down, Viktor is once again acting like a cold fish. I think that he is keeping his distance. Do you want to meet up and pour out our grief for a bit?"

"Of course, don't feel upset though. I walk to Kugulu Park after I leave home. And we can meet up there if you leave now, alright?"

"Okay, see you."

Galina understood the cipher message. For Mariya to convey the message she has got in emergency situations to Galina, she was calling Galina and used phrases involving negativity such as "I'm a little upset" as a meeting code which meant that they had to meet immediately.

Even though she was unmasked about which she hadn't informed SVR, she was not neglecting the instructions that were sent to her and was acting as if everything had been normal. Galina was a traitor to SVR now!

Galina quickly left home. When she was approaching the park, she saw that Mariya was sitting on a bench, holding a water bottle. Galina walked to Mariya. Mariya stood up the moment she saw her. They kissed each other and said hi.

"Let's walk, shall we?" Mariya asked.

"Alright," Galina replied.

While they were walking, Mariya whispered to her, "There's going to be a vital summit in the first week of the following month. John is among the invited guests. However, we're out of this meeting. John is going to attend the meeting just like other diplomats, wearing a voice recording device and deliver the documents, information, and recordings that he obtains to the USA embassy after one day to not attract notice. We need to copy these records on the day of the meeting. But the voice recorder is a cryptographic device that was produced by the CIA. Therefore, it will take time to decrypt.

The participants and the public are generally informed two months before the summit. But this one is not ordinary. Obviously, there is an emergency. Probably, a civil war to break out in Turkey or the refugee problem of Turkey arising out of the war and the intense conflict in neighboring countries will be evaluated. Since we are also a neighboring country, this summit is the most important task. Therefore, we need to reach the details of the subject. The meeting will be confidential. The UN Turkish Representation will host the summit. I'll tell you about more when you come to the gym. But you need to obtain the voice recording device at any cost. This is all for now," she ended her words.

Then Galina said, "Copy that."

After walking for a while, they entered a bookstore and started to examine the books.

Mariya said, "Look at this one."

Galina took the book. She looked at the contents of the book and read through a few pages. In the book, the theses of the President of Kazakhstan, Nursultan Nazarbayev, on the unification of Turkish states were explained.

"Galina! Look at this section. The slant-eyed Kazakhs are still planning something about their relatives here and in Central Asia. The Turanian ideology is still causing trouble to the Five in the UN Security Council. In fact, it would be more correct to say the biggest trouble."

"Even though the Soviet assimilation that lasted 70 years, the topic is still on the agenda."

"Let me show you a book." After looking carefully at the bookshelves, she took another book. She pointed a paragraph after reading through a few pages. "Please read here."

Galina read the lines;

"Do not worry, take your time, remember,

Do not step out of the line in season and out of season,

Do not boil over before the pot starts boiling,

The world will be ours, either today or tomorrow.

The time is of Tabriz, and the world is of the power,

The road is of God, and the world is of justice and rights.

Ultimately, the world is of Turks.

No matter three or five days, it will happen sooner or later,

The world will be ours, either today or tomorrow.

The new order and the new extent is Qur'an.

Our first word and our last are Turan.

It is the Prophet and the Qur'an, delivering the message.

"Whatever is going to happen, is for the better."

After taking a deep breath, Galina said, "It is necessary to bring these movements under control."

Then they left the bookstore after examining a few novels. They decided to walk to the end of the street.

They were looking at the retail displays of the shops as they walked. Mariya said to Galina, "Is there an increase in the pace of work at the UN?"

"Nothing out of the ordinary."

"Particularly observe whether John is stressed, acting out of his character, and is increasing his pace compared to normal; this is vital..."

"Okay. I will ask those in the department on the sly whether there's an increase in the load of works during the lunch hour and returns."

*

Galina called John on Sunday, saying, "John, if you are available, I want to cook something nice and come to you."

John replied, "Okay."

Obviously, Galina hadn't cooked something. She entered the picnic-style place on the side of the road before she went to his home. After getting two baked jacket potatoes, she headed to John's house. When John opened the door, he was expecting that Galina would be holding a food container or a pot.

Galina kissed John on his mouth.

"John, how are you?"

"Just fine, thanks. What about you?"

"For some reason, I feel quite sluggish. That's why I couldn't cook for you but bought baked jacket potatoes since I know that you love them."

"Thank you so much. Then let's eat before they get cold."

"Alright, but I feel so tired, would you get a spoon from the kitchen? I don't feel like going to work tomorrow, I hope it won't be a busy week."

"Something tells me the next few weeks will be intense."

"It can't be."

John ate his food quite fast. He took his laptop, sat on the single seat, and turned on his laptop, typing his 25-digit password. He was always turning on his laptop on the single seat while Galina was around. Galina would not go over John and pretend to respect his work with many secret elements; she would not even go by his side.

*

Galina spent her all week watching her department co-workers and her co-workers in other departments. Decent observation and quick decision-making were among the most important traits of her. While transferring her observations to Mariya, Galina stated that the works were gaining speed at the

Humanitarian Coordination Office, the UN Population Fund and World Food Program Offices, the World Health Organization, and the International Organization for Migration. At the same time, she told her that John had looked quite tired and that when she called John, he said that he had had some works to do and that he would call her later.

Galina told Mariya, "You seem to be very stressed, by the way."

"Me?" Mariya asked herself.

Galina sensed that there were some quick changes and things were not going quite well. The tension inside her was growing rapidly. She did not want to ask Mariya questions as she was afraid of being misunderstood. There was no place to make mistakes and to tolerate mistakes even among themselves in this job. The slightest doubt might cause her to find herself in the Lubyanka Prison in Moscow.

Mariya told Galina, "You may need to kill John."

"Why?"

"I don't know why, but I can guess."

"Method?"

"Not clear, still being evaluated. Prepare yourself. When the instruction is received, you have to end this as soon as possible."

Galina closed her eyes as if saying okay.

While on the way home, Galina was thinking of methods that she needed to utilize. Since John's house might be watched by different services due to extraordinary activity, she decided to do that out of his house. Was he going to be killed explicitly, or was it going to be made look like a suicide? The reason for the greatest question mark in her mind was that.

In cases where he was killed explicitly, a message would be given to the institution where John was associated with. What was this message? While thinking about them, she thought that the headquarters were acting gawkishly; if John was a target to be killed, this had to be planned and prepared beforehand, and operations that had been planned suddenly might turn into disasters. Then she consoled herself, "Maybe they will cancel it at the last minute."

When she came home, she was so exhausted that when Doruk called her, he asked, "Galina... Have you been sleeping?"

When Doruk went home, he realized that she was rather confused. He told Galina, "For whatever reason, I haven't seen you well, you're so thoughtful and lifeless." "I am a little tired," Galina replied.

John crossed Doruk's mind, instead of Galina's risky and dangerous job. He was actually jealous of Galina from him. Galina was meeting with John on the days when she refused to meet with him. Doruk was unable to bring himself to this, even though he was aware of John even before meeting with Galina. He was feeling sorry for Galina because of her traumas and the fact that he used Galina.

"A person can love someone who he
pities easier than someone who he envies. "

Andre Maurois

Was Doruk stuck between pity and hatred? Did he fall in love with Galina? He considered his feelings as masculine feelings and ignored them. He was avoiding confronting himself.

Galina was trying to pretend that she was not thoughtful at the dinner and to act as if she had been cheerful and was talking about her co-workers.

The next day was one of the routine days on which she went to the gym. She was looking for to meeting Mariya at the gym.

When she went to the gym, she entered straight into the locker room and changed her clothes. After tying her hair up, she went to Mariya who was sitting at the small cafeteria and said, "Hi Mariya, I feel quite dynamic today, I'll start immediately." She positioned herself in front of the mirror and started performing warming-up exercises. Mariya said to her quietly, "Delete John's hard disk no later than one week." This was the order to kill John. Galina glassily nodded.

After finishing her usual exercises in the gym in compliance with her schedule, she took a shower and left. On leaving, Mariya gave a thermos to Galina, saying, "I guess you've forgotten this here." Realizing that there were instructions and tools needed for the operation in that thermos, she put it immediately in her bag, and replied, "Thank you, I was constantly looking for this in my bag."

She opened the thermos as soon as she went home. The moment she finished her examination, she called John. They decided to meet at a far east restaurant in the evening.

Galina came to the restaurant before John. After eating their dinners quietly and cozily, "John, red days are ahead. I suggest you enjoy this deprivation," Galina laughed.

When they got home, Galina took the ice from the refrigerator and put it on the table in the living room. When she went back into the kitchen, a sound of shattering glass was heard. "Is everything okay?" John asked.

"We have only one bottle of mineral water left."

"Let me call the shop, they will bring a bottle of coke."

"I decided to drink it straight tonight. And you seem to have put on some weight. It would be better for you if you drank it with mineral water."

"It's because I'm exercising irregularly, not because of the whiskey and coke."

"The red river may flow any minute, do not be deprived of me for the sake of the coke!"

Galina took the mineral water bottle along with the lid opener and the whiskey bottle in the showcase in the living room. She poured the whiskey straight into her glass and poured whiskey and mineral water into John's glass. Galina proposed a toast, saying, "To happiness."

When they drank their first sip, Galina made a wry face, saying, "That's hard."

While Galina was pouring their second glass of whiskey, she emptied the mineral water bottle into her glass. "Don't do that, it was mine," John complained. Galina ignored John with a feminine smile and poured straight whiskey into John's glass.

Galina told John, "The first day I saw you, I thought that you were pretty cool and unapproachable. It was obvious from the outside that you were unachievable." John was listening to Galina with an undefinable joy. As Galina paid compliments to John, he was getting drunker and drunker. Galina glorified him, saying, "It is a rare condition for such a charming and sexy man to be successful at the same time, this is why I consider myself lucky, luckily I have you."

Galina's confessions were followed by John's compliments. As John told Galina, "You connected me to life," he sipped the last glass of straight whiskey.

John was about to pass out.

When Galina finished her glass, she started kissing John. Suddenly she told John, "Your mouth is sour due to straight whiskey, I told you, we should have bought a bottle of coke." Then she stood up and picked the pink round coated candy that was sold in the markets out of her bag and opened its cap. After taking some for herself, she treated to John. John was so drunk that he was unable to get his hand into the small container. Galina gave three candies to John in her hand. "Come on, bite them!" Galina said.

After John consumed all the candies, they continued kissing. Galina opened the other whiskey bottle that was in the showcase and gave him another glass. John dropped the glass on himself. His pants were dripping whiskey. Now he had only one desire, to take off Galina's blouse. But Galina was not allowing him to do so in no way. John became obsessed with Galina's blouse.

As Galina unbuttoned John's pants, he was still trying to unbutton Galina's blouse. Suddenly, Galina bit her lower lip with her teeth and shook her head, saying, "Hmmm...." She poured whiskey into John's glass again and passed it to his lips. John took a few more sips, spilling some drops on himself. Galina was looking at the clock as she was counting the minutes for the drug to take effect. It was time.

Galina held his hand and took him to the bedroom. After taking off John's pants, she sat down on him. John was not able to speak anymore, and his eyes were weary. He was touched by Galina's love moans as always. Galina kept going upside down on John. At the same time, she was kissing John and hugging him tightly.

When John climaxed, Galina told John, "Look, I'm taking off my blouse."

John saw the picture of her mother laying in blood without her head attached on Galina's breasts. John had no choice but to have a heart attack.

Nobody ever thought that the pictures of John's mother on social media would cause so much trouble. In order to ensure the impression that he had been doing ecstasy during the autopsy, Galina had drugged his food with the ecstasy pills sold in Turkey and kept adding the ecstasy dust to his drink. After giving the ecstasy pills looked like candies in the candy container to John, he eventually had a heart attack as he felt the terror which quickly changed his mood during orgasm under the influence of alcohol.

Galina kept going up and down and hugging him as he was shaking uncontrollably. Then she laid down next to John as if nothing had happened. John died shakingly. If this plan was not successful, she would have to break his neck in the bathtub and make it looked like a suicide. It was not easy to break the neck. At least for Galina. She was happy that she did not have to do so. After making sure that John was dead, she decided to sleep. She took a deep breath.

"The thief and the murderer follow nature just as much as the philanthropist."

Thomas Henry Huxley

It was 9:30 am when Galina woke up. She called the police and asked for an ambulance.

How John was to be killed was a hard-studied plan. Galina had once told John that she had wanted to shave John with his razor, that she had seen that in a movie, and that she had been unable to get it out of mind and had persuaded him. She had told him that the guy was wearing a towel around his waist and she had liked that, but she had postponed shaving after the shower, telling that John was attractive enough for her and so that John's skin wouldn't get loose and resistant to the razor. While she had shaved him, she had pushed it a little bit hard and cut his chin. Then she had taken the razor and the cotton that John had pressed on his wound and put them in her bag.

She had dumped the open razor in her bag and the tiny cotton piece to the trash can next to the toilet by applying nail polish on it.

In addition, she had sent her night robe after covering it with John's bodily fluids to the headquarters. Most importantly, she had picked a couple of strands of his hair and put them into her purse. Moreover, she had stolen one of John's undershirt for his scent. Stealing clothes for scent was one of the heritages of East Germany Ministry for State Security (also known as Stasi or Ministerium für Staatssicherheit) that came down to KBG (also known as Committee for State Security or Komitet Gosudarstvennoy Bezopasnosti). That heritage now was being used by FSB (also known as Federalnaya Sluzhba Bezopasnosti or Russian Federal Security Service-Internal Intelligence) and SVR.

Triggering allergic reaction through anaphylactic shock and causing narrowing and blockage in the trachea was another method of assassination. That was one of the best methods. Because it was not always possible to find the causes of sudden deaths that occurred because of this method. However, this method was not always proven to be effective. It was found from the data Galina had sent the headquarters that John had cyst hydatid allergy which was not common in daily life. Therefore, this method was not used.

Galina ensured that they thought that he had a reaction due to intoxication by stating that while they had eaten at the restaurant, something had clogged his throat and he had had to cough. For this reason, an autopsy was decided to be performed. If an autopsy was done, nothing more than ecstasy would appear and the suspicions on Galina would come to an end. When the policed asked for the camera records of the restaurant, they learned that the restaurant had no interior cameras and had two separate cameras where the valet received the car, which made things quite difficult. Mariya had suggested Galina two restaurants in which they had no cameras. They learned that they did not have cameras inside when Mariya went to the restaurant a few days prior and asked for the camera records in exchange for money, claiming that her husband had been cheating on him.

*

The murder of John had many important consequences on several counts. The Syrian war had to be suspended until a new appointment was made. In this way, Russia was able to send more ammunition and air defense systems to Syria.

In addition, the evaluations of Turkey on matters such as how many refugees and how many shelters Turkey could afford, in which airports, ports, and the country that the medical teams, the vaccine and drug boxes, and the translator would be deployed were left half finished. In addition to this purpose, Turkey-UN relations would break down due to the suspicion that John was poisoned by Turkey while he was eating outside and therefore the USA would need to re-analyze the possible changes in Turkey's behavior. The analyzes also required diplomatic negotiations. All this meant time. Even an hour during the days on the edge of a war outbreak was vital.

*

Galina mourned for about a month after John's mortal remains were sent back home after the autopsy. She went to her workplace wearing dark clothes and no makeup. Even though newspaper wrote that John had died because of a heart attack, it was spoken that John had been killed in the UN.

Galina was acting as if she was drowning among the rumors. All eyes were on Galina. She had not neglected to go to a psychiatrist and have medications prescribed.

This was why she was more cautious during her meetings with Doruk.

A few months later, she was relieved with the message given by Mariya. Mariya told her that she had decided to resign to live in Moscow. "What did you feel and what did you want to do when you saw John's dead body?" Mariya asked Galina.

"I felt unhappy that I lost one of my sources and that I was not able to enjoy kissing my other source at length after performing oral sex on the first one. I would want to watch the body after waiting for it for a while as the flies seize their places on the body and as the maggots start to devour the body..."

So, who would maintain contact with Doruk? That was what was important to Galina.

CHAPTER THREE
THE END

While she was thinking that she would be appointed to Central Asia, Galina was quite happy when she found out that she would be working in SVR Headquarters in Moscow.

She was wearing a collared white shirt, a black skirt, and a gray jacket on the first day of her work. The knot which was done by the hairdresser at the early hours of the morning suited her quite well. She was ready for the first day at work.

Since she came back from Turkey hurriedly and she was unable to buy her managers gifts from Turkey, she visited some shops in which Turkish brands were sold in Moscow. She bought her manager a nice shirt and a tie. When she entered the room of her manager, he stood up and said, "Welcome, Galina."

After telling about Turkey in general, Galina gave the Turkish-made shirt and the tie to her manager after mentioning that she had bought them in Moscow. Her manager laughingly said, "I hope wearing clothes from Turkey which is our occasional ally won't cause any troubles. Galina smiled.

The headquarters looked like somewhere well-disciplined. Actually, it was unfavorable for Galina to work straight at the headquarters. Because Turks and the USA after investigating the murder of John might follow her in Moscow. But the autopsy had dropped the subject. However, Galina was still checking whether she was being followed or not. She never encountered something that would cause suspicion.

The headquarters were quite boring than the field. All the women here were rather well-groomed. The women had nothing other than themselves to invest, inasmuch as they could not afford to invest. The only investment they had made was their beautiful and attractive clothes, their well-cared nails, and fragrant perfumes. All those women only had one dream; to meet a rich businessman or an oligarch and to live without working.

*

Galina failed to stop thinking about Doruk. Doruk was constantly texting to Galina. Galina's manager told her that she would be in contact with Doruk herself.

Galina was being trained on cryptography on one hand, and on the other hand, she was dealing with the translation of documents, information etc. that had been provided by their personnel in Turkey. There were so many sources that Galina and her co-workers were translating these documents until midnight.

Galina started to dream in Turkish while she was sleeping.

Her mother could not stand her tiredness. One time, she wanted her to rest well and she did not wake her up in the morning. When Galina went to work, she came across with her manager's sullen face at first and then she had to explain why she was late to work.

*

Galina had to answer Doruk's meeting requests and to meet with him now. The most important point was the effect of the rendezvous point to the consequence of the task.

Because a not-well-planned rendezvous point had resulted in the failure of many important tasks. Doruk stated a few times that she had missed Galina. They decided to meet in Italy.

Doruk bought a tour named "Four-day Italy."

Before Doruk hit the road, he had drawn the ballistic missile projects that he had kept in his mind, on a paper. He had to draw and present that well. Probably, Galina would be secretly recording the drawing and the presentation. Long-range domestic and national missile undoubtedly would haunt Russians in their dreams. There was nothing more natural than countries presenting themselves stronger than they were.

After settling into the hotel with Doruk who came to Italy, she asked while she was taking the tour in the lobby, "I want to hang out by myself for a bit, is there a live porn theater pub here just like in Germany? The tour guide answered, "I guess not." Doruk was not neglecting to behave as if he was a single tourist.

Doruk gave the name of the hotel after getting into a taxi at the entrance of the hotel. He entered the room that was booked by SVR under his name. There was still three hours for Galina to come. He took a shower. There might a camera in his room. He could not check that.

To surprise Galina, Doruk called the room service and asked for napkins. Since the napkins delivered were low in quantity, he asked a couple more from the room service attendant. He seemed confused but he smilingly said, "With pleasure."

Doruk decided to lay down on the bed without taking off his trousers, close his eyes, and take a nap. He startled the moment he heard the knock on the door.

When he opened the door, he gave approximately 20 roses made from napkins with the bouquet that was also made from napkins to Galina. Doruk said, "I'm sorry that I could not get you flowers, but I made these." Galina entered the room and kissed Doruk so many times that it was maybe over ten.

Doruk was also quite happy.

After some bed-fun, Doruk took a shower. He was thinking in the shower, "We would have disgraced ourselves if the camera captured us." "We have not much time. If you give what you wanted to give to me now, I'll deliver it to my friend next-door," Galina said. Doruk took the laptop and the large papers folded from his bag which was near Galina. He started drawing.

When the drawing was over, Doruk whimpered, "I would not believe that if they had told me that one day I would be dealing with engineering."

Galina folded the papers. Then she put them in a thin file. Before she took the file and left the room, she knocked on the wall three times. When she left the room, there was someone who also left the room next-door and Galina gave the file to her neighbor in the elevator.

After asking the receptionist where the most delicious spaghetti was made by showing the receptionist the city guide. While the front office attendant was showing and marking the restaurant on the city map, he was examining the features of Galina. The happiness that Doruk had given to Galina was apparently obvious.

They had their breakfast in a cafe that was within walking distance of the hotel. Since they spontaneously decided to sit there, they were talking quite freely. Doruk was telling Galina that how he had missed her and the times he wandered around on the street on which Galina's former apartment had been. And Galina was telling him that how she hated her job, her workplace, and Moscow. She was listing how people in Moscow talking dirty, how they were disrespectful, and all the negative qualities of them. Doruk thought to himself, "How could a person hate her people, her capital that much?" He was taking notes of the details in his mind to tell when he would get back to Ankara.

*

Doruk looked quite tired when he returned to Ankara. Murat said to him, "Stress tires a man." Ahmet said, glancing at him cunningly, "He fucks, and he complains!" Murat replied to him, "It's his job now."

Doruk told his managers all the details. His manager told him, "I've got an idea on my mind, but I need to talk to my superiors first."

Many thoughts crossed Doruk's mind while he was leaving the room. Would he share these ideas with him? Or wait for his manager's offer? When he sat on his desk, he was evaluating his ideas.

*

Doruk would never leave home without having a proper breakfast. When he sat on his desk, he would drink a Turkish coffee first and then start working. His inferior co-workers would come late to work and enjoy their breakfast for a long time.

His phone rang. It was his manager. Doruk answered the phone, "Yes, sir?" "Doruk, would you please come to the meeting room?" His manager asked.

When he went to the meeting room, he saw that all his superiors were there. Doruk knew that it was an extraordinary situation when he saw that many superior officers were ready at the meeting room.

His manager took the word, "As you know; our allies, threat perceptions, and the goals of regional and global terror elements accordingly have been constantly changing. But we also develop multi-dimensional strategies. Turkey is a great country now. It has a vital role in the world. It has the qualification and the opportunity to change the destiny of the world. Furthermore, the world cannot be ruled alone by 5 members of the United Nations that have veto power. You'll see, we will make a breakthrough by saying "The World is Bigger than Five." While politicians are re-designing the world, we are working on the possible effects of the intelligence trade with 5 countries that have veto power and the countries that are in the list of these 5 countries after the breakthrough, and we develop a vision. We are aiming to get into a game whose details will be provided to you later. Your role here is to ensure by persuading Galina that she marries to a superior officer of SVR whether single or married. In this way, we are going to perform great operations through Galina who hates her country. Are you feeling ready?" He finished his words.

Doruk replied, "I'm always ready."

Doruk was excited but he was also determined.

When he got onto the plane to Baku, he was flying in CIP section. The flight attendant stirred Doruk's tea and even closed the sun-shields so that the sun would not bother Doruk. Doruk thought to himself, "This is why I prefer Azerbaijan Airways." There was an enormous service quality. Nearly half of the movies that were provided to him were on Armenians' genocide towards Azerbaijanis. Doruk said to himself, "I've already watched these movies a lot. Why not enjoy my flight?" And he started to watch an old comedy movie.

It was his first time in Azerbaijan. He felt like he was at home. He met a Georgian-origin taxi driver. He saved his phone number. Mamuko was speaking Azerbaijan Turkish quite well. He was also guiding Doruk. His car was rather old, but Doruk was having much fun. Mamuko said, "There was Kenan, right?" Kenan the restaurant owner. He used to gamble here and lost all of his money, then he traveled with the richest Russian women, he was siphoning those women, a lot." in Azerbaijan Turkish. Doruk was thinking to himself, "What an enjoyable gossiper." "I should ask for my abroad appointment in Baku, it's a place to live." Doruk whimpered.

Galina had started to wander around before he met Doruk. She was examining the books in a bookstore she had entered. She was also looking at outside to check whether someone was following her or not. But there was no one. Then she suddenly startled. A man instantly approached her and said to her in Russian,

"I can help you if you are looking for a specific book."

"I was looking for freshly released novels."

"At this section."

"Thanks."

While she was doing her routine checks, she once started to take a glance at the outside through the showcase. She walked a few steps. Then she picked another book. And turned its back. She started to read a random page in the book. A sentence that she read excited her attention. As she was evaluating the sentence on her mind, she came to the exit. She was sure that she was not being followed.

After Doruk met with Galina and they fulfilled their longing, he told her about Mamuko. They laughed together. Then Mamuko took them for a barbecue at the buoyant water which was at the upstate. It was a little bit commonplace, but the dishes were quite well, and the water was rather healing as told by Mamuko. "What's this?" Doruk asked the waiter. The waiter said, "Cilantro herb." "It has a different taste, tho," Doruk replied. The waiter smiled.

While they were in the puddle, "Galina, I do not want to demoralize you, but the National Intelligence Service increased the pressure on me. They want me to meet with you at least twice a month and deliver fake projects and documents to you and they are also asking for a way to meet with you whenever they want. Otherwise, they told me that we would put me in a solitary cell." Doruk said.

"The other way?" Galina asked. "They want to you marry to a superior officer who you'll meet in SVR, to become lovers if he's married, to promote faster, and to convey all the high-confidential information to their side. They also stated that they will provide you with full support. For example; they will provide you with the bribe which will enable you to work in the same environment with the target to change your department, and if the target is married, they will provide you with support for him to be divorced." He continued.

Galina let herself down in the water. But it was not letting you sink. When she got out of the water, she approached Doruk. She wiped her eyes with her hand. Mamuko had stated that the water was harmful to eyes.

"I'm sick of these blackmails and requests, Doruk. Both sides have no rules. It would be our disaster if we met every other two-weeks. If you keep getting out of your country to meet me and if your country does not step in, they will immediately find out that I'm engaged."

"Galina, I really have no other choice than this. How many times I wanted to kill myself..."?

"Let's drop it."

"Look! If you feel uncomfortable, go to Turkey back and tell them I blackmailed you."

"Do you want both of us to get killed?"

Doruk hanged his head. Galina went outside and applied a face-mask just like other women. There was not even a sunbed to lay down. She stood for a while and turned her face to the sun. Then they sat at some place resembling an estaminet.

Galina told that she would get out of the taxi at the beginning of the street on which her hotel was. While she was walking with Doruk before entering the hotel, "I'll send the copies of the documents you gave to the Russian Embassy here. Controls in the airports are quite tight, it is not what it used to be. Their hatred towards Russia in their subconscious makes it harder for us to operate. The forced togetherness in the Commonwealth of Independent States caused displeasure rather than establishing tight and warm relations." She informed him.

Galina called somewhere with a fixed-line telephone. "Is taxi alright?" She asked in Russian. After receiving the answer, Galina hung up the phone, saying, "I'm sorry, wrong number." Within 20 minutes, somebody whose face Doruk could not see came into the room and took away the documents.

Doruk realized that SVR was operating more freely in Azerbaijan than in Italy. Was the reason for that they had much more sources in the Azerbaijan Secret Service? Or were they sure that both Galina and Doruk were not being followed? Otherwise, he would not have come into the room directly. However, the fact that they cared for Doruk not to see the courier's face might mean that they had some question marks on their mind towards Doruk.

Galina was rather thoughtful. Doruk was quietly watching TV for her to think freely. He did not forget that he had to appear a little bit pale and sad.

After the sunset, "Let's eat outside, shall we, Doruk? Galina asked.

"Alright, sure."

Baku evenings were wonderful. They went to a beautiful restaurant. After the dishes were over, "Let's walk for a while, so we could burn the calories." Galina proposed.

They started walking. "Tell them to send me fifty thousand dollars. The courier who will carry the money must come to the Church of Holy Prophet Elijah on the following Sunday. And he must put the money in a box resembling those candle boxes. He must approach me by pointing there. We'll approach the donation box and donate. I'll take a glance to the priest and smile. Probably he will come to us. Then he will perform a ceremony. While he was performing the ceremony, our faces will be looking at the entrance and the priest clothes will cover our front. When the priest prays and closes his eyes, I'll change the boxes with my foot. He'll push his to me and I'll push mine to him. Thus, I'll take the box to home as if I am going to light a candle." She explained. "Okay, I'll tell them." Doruk continued.

Galina excitedly reawaken the subject, "Doruk, I've heard that Azerbaijani doctors are experts on the test-tube baby and that they opened many test-tube baby centers in Moscow." Waiting for this proposal for a long time, Doruk offered, "Let's go to a center tomorrow and I'll give my sperm." Galina told him that she had not made an appointment yet but if they bribe them, they would give priority to them. Doruk liked that idea.

The next day, Doruk picked Galina from the hotel. Since Galina had been way too tired and wanted to get rest well, she had wanted to sleep alone. Doruk was sweating a lot while he was sleeping. For this reason, Galina had told Doruk many times that he should have checked it up.

They went to a test-tube baby center together.

"Hi, we are coming from Turkey and we don't have an appointment," Doruk said and left 20 Manats on the secretary's desk. The secretary took the money and put it in her drawer, then locked it. She raised his head and smiled, saying "You need to fill this tube before talking to a doctor."

The secretary accompanying Doruk told him, "You may use this room." Doruk went in. The secretary knocked on the door, saying, "I'm so sorry, I guess I forgot to turn on the TV. She turned on the TV. The television was showing an old video. The porn film appeared on the TV. Doruk locked the door. He unbuttoned his pants. He was so concentrated on the film that he forgot to take off his belt. He took off his belt. Doruk would never go outside without a belt. A belt could be used as a weapon when necessary.

Galina was getting bored of waiting. When Doruk came out, she said, "Why did it take so long, did you cheat on me, is this why?" Galina asked.

"No, I loved a part of the film, and I watched it again."

"What was that nice part?"

"The official chauffeur was fucking the wife of his boss. Same to me."

Doruk was following a method in which he insulted, swore, criticized, and despised his superiors. He was so focused on this method that while he was talking to his managers, he was accidentally using adjectives such as "the bastard manager." Moreover, the movie that he had watched was not even similar to his explanation of the movie. The movie took place in a modern brothel.

Doruk gave the sperm-filled tube to the nurse. After a quick examination, they talked to the doctor. "You have left your contact information, correct? We'll get back at you and start the procedures afterward," the doctor said. "Yes, we have," Galina replied. Galina had written false information such as false names, surnames, and phone numbers on the form. She had thought to herself, "If we come to Baku once again, we'll get back here or Doruk will contact them on phone."

*

Doruk prepared his report when he got back to Turkey. He mentioned all the details, even the name of the movie, in his report.

There were no issues of trust towards Doruk, apparently. Even so, Doruk was writing his reports quite detailed and was ruling out possible question marks. Because Ahmet was still picking on Doruk.

When he went to his manager's room to deliver the report, "Why does Ahmet love you that much?" His manager asked.

"Sir, I do not think that Ahmet loves me that much, but if so, I don't know why," Doruk replied surprisingly.

"I wanted to ask about his opinion in one subject and he told me that you would know it the best." He explained.

"I'm glad that I have heard that. I hope I won't leave Ahmet in the lurch." Doruk answered.

"I asked one of the veterans about it, no worries."

"While he was studying in the university, Ahmet bought a postpaid line under the name of his mother and couldn't pay for it when the bill came. He checked the mailbox every day so that his mother would not see the bill and he was paying for it partially. When they went to their summer house, his expenses increased and thus, he was unable to pay the bill. Therefore, the line was interrupted, and he continued to use his old prepaid line."

"And..." (Looking at Doruk straight in the eye)

"Then the operator sent a written notice under his mother name to his mother's house. In the notice, it was stated that the debt had to be paid to the given bank account; otherwise, necessary executions would take place. Ahmet contacted a lawyer and paid for a part of it. At the end of the year, the lawyer covered for small amounts in his cases so that he would get better grades in his performance evaluation and get as many execution files as possible. While doing so, he sent money to Ahmet's account. Ahmet gave this money to his mother who sent it to the lawyer's account.

In the inquiry, when the account activities were evaluated, this complicated issue came to surface, and they asked Ahmet to contact the lawyer. However, the lawyer was in Diyarbakir with his family as her wife was delivering their baby at that time of the year. Ahmet found a chance to introduce himself to the lawyer as if he was a brother of a doctor in the hospital and as if he was an Information and Communication Technologies specialist and established a conversation with him on common grounds.

It is known that the Information and Communication Technologies Authority imposes a penalty on GSM operators.

One thing led to another and Ahmet asked, "Was your office on Tunali Hilmi Street?" And told him that Ahmet had been his uncle's son which had contacted him and had had a bill under his mother's name. The lawyer recalled the issue and told him that he had paid it himself.

Upon this, when we met Ahmet in the lunchtime and I told this story by saying, "May God give the best of the lawyers" and everyone on the table laughed, and Ahmet lost his face. No other matter."

"I have never heard such an execution case." His manager laughed.

*

When Galina came back to Moscow, she was acting hurriedly, saying "I've got so much to do." She went to his co-worker Katya, "I've got something on my mind that bugs me. There might be a relation between two events, can I ask you to list the robberies against Tatars in Crimea? I would be glad if you put it on my desk." She asked. Katya said to her, "Of course."

When Galina got back to her desk, she found an enormous file.

Galina examined the robberies that took place during the years she had been working. Then she delivered the documents to Katya. "Take a look at it if you want to, I thought that I could find some relations, but I failed to do so." She told her. "Let me take a look," Katya said and took the file.

Galina used Katya to get what she wanted without having to research about Crimea on her own system.

*

Galina went straight to the church from her house. While she was going to the church, she checked multiple times whether she was being followed or not. It seemed that she was not being followed. When she reached the church, a white-yellow skinned lady with brown eyes approached her and said, "I've got your box." The woman was resembling Russians with her tip-tilted beautiful nose, was not offending the eye, was not drawing attention, and was not actually resembling Russians when she was examined closely.

Galina thought that she was probably from Ukraine. "A mixed-blood, obviously." She said. What did she have to with Turks? She thought as she sat down on her chair. The woman sat a chair that was a little bit far away. Galina was waiting for the priest to approach as she tried to figure out how she was doing business with Turks. For a moment, she whimpered to herself, "Like you don't collaborate with them; in this case either she is against the system or she is doing this for money. Maybe she is a Gagauz Turk."

They changed their boxes as planned. Galina went to her house after leaving the church. She had no choice but to hide the money in her room.

She was looking forward to the next day. She called the Associate Director Nikolay who was responsible for personnel relations and asked for an appointment. The appointment was 11:00 on the next day.

Galina woke up early in the morning and took for a walk. She took a shower, then she got ready. When she looked at the mirror, she was getting more aware of the light in her eyes.

She went to her appointment five minutes early. After ten minutes, she went into the room of the Associate Director. As Nikolay was examining a file that he was holding, he looked at Galina over his glasses. He pointed the chair with his hand and started talking, "I'm listening. It seems that you came here without your unit manager's permission. Our door is open to all of our personnel, but only for three minutes for those coming without permission."

Galina immediately cut in on. "I want to be transferred to the American Department where I think that I'll be productive much more. My field experience is quite enough. I believe that I'm good at interpreting and analyze people and events. As far as I can see, my file is right in front of you. If you are available, I would like to invite you to Metropol Restaurant where my mother has worked." Galina said. Nikolay's cold face expression turned into a smile and sincerity, and said, "I'll see you at 20 hundred." Galina left the room with joy, saying, "I'll see you there."

She took a cab as soon as she left her workplace to get ready for the evening. She did herself a favor because taking a taxi was expensive. She thought to herself, "I'll also use the money which Doruk had it provided."

Nikolay was at the restaurant just on time. Galina was sitting on the table which she had booked in the afternoon as if she was the host. Her mother had worked there for a couple years. Nikolay launched forth with a question, "Is your mother, Darya, still working here? "She left a couple years ago, but she is still good friends with the chef," Galina answered.

After ordering their dishes, Galina told him about her work in Crimea and Turkey with the main lines. She told him that she had revealed the thief gang that had stolen fur-coats in the market-square coincidentally by scrutinizing Tatars in Crimea.

She said, "I received some money for rainy days from this gang. But I want to use this money in my career, not to let it wait for rainy days."

"Alright, but do you want to change your department, or do you want to be the manager of the department to which you'll be transferred?" Nikolay asked.

"I just want to change my department for now and to prove myself there," Galina answered.

"How many fur-coats do you have for that?" Nikolay asked. "Twenty-five thousand dollars for this. But also, I have the same fund for the personality analysis of the unit manager, Grigoriy, whose name is mentioned in the Associate Directorship." She answered.

"It makes sense if you're going to try to get promoted together, the new generation is very productive, to be honest."

"I'll call Gregoriy and have him open a personnel request. We'll meet here on the following Monday at the same time. Get a chess board and put the money in there. And give it to me here. And I'll give you a small study with the title "Promotion Principles in Departments." You'll open it and read Grigoriy."

"Deal."

They made a toast for "health."

*

Galina put the file in her bag as soon as she received it. She finished her dinner. And she left the table. Galina felt fear while she was thinking that it was not surprising for Nikolay to be fearless and brave to send his driver to a restaurant that was in the middle of Moscow to receive the money. Nikolay was also smart enough to validate the information about the robberies in Crimea, which was provided by Galina, before getting into that water. He checked whether her mother had worked there, as well. It was maybe because of the occupation or to come to the restaurant perpetually. Who knew? Galina had been used to deal with the results rather than reasons from the first day she had started working in SVR.

When she came home, she went through Gregoriy's file. Grigoriy was such a clinical case... His mother had left him and his father, married to a tailor and settled in Petersburg. His aunt, Kseniya had started to take care of Grigoriy when he was four years old. Kseniya had brought up Grigoriy separately from her own son, Andrey. Andrey had been very jealous of Grigoriy who was one year older than him. Andrey had been such a jealous boy that he had not allowed Kseniya to take Grigoriy on her lap in the one-room house.

Grigoriy's poor father had sent him to a military school to put him off. He was remembering his relationship with his mother indistinctly. When he had graduated from the military school, he had found his mother and paid a visit to her. These visits were going on occasionally.

His disrupted family order and the challenges of the military school caused severe damages in his psychology. Since Girgoriy had been brought up without motherly love, he had a rather sad personality. It was stated in his file that he had been creating problems that would cause him to be unhappy.

"If motherly love is there, it is like a blessing; if it is not there, itis as if all beauty had gone out of life—and there is nothing I can do to create it"

Erich Fromm

Galina knew that the medications that Grigoriy used were quite heavy. "How could a man have sex while on these pills?" She thought to herself. And the subject was sex once again. His file consisted of his discipline punishments, his good friends, his first girlfriend, his ex-wife, his ex-lovers in the service, places where he hired prostitutes, his favorite gun, his cigarette brand, his favorite car, his favorite liqueur, his favorite dishes, his favorite writers, his style, his cloth preference, his favorite brands, his certificates of achievement, and his medals, etc.

Galina kept reading the file quickly. The appointment order would be given tomorrow, and she had to meet with Grigoriy. It had been mentioned that he had the brightest future and he had been filling his pockets the most during his tasks. Grigoriy had the two elements combined. Money and success. Which one was important for him more than SVR? Success? Or money? It did not matter much. Success always brought money along.

Galina read the file second time. During this, her mother knocked on the door and called out, "Gala..." "Mom, can you excuse me for a while?" Galina asked and left her room. She went to the bathroom and threw the whole file that she had torn apart and flushed.

*

Galina went into the Grigoriy's room.

Grigoriy looked at Galina and said, "You are the privileged one of Mr. Nikolay, I guess." This statement was not a nice way to welcome someone.

"Yes, it is me."

"I have examined your file. I have also thought that you could contribute to our unit."

"Before you meet your co-workers, there is a sensitive subject that we have been working on."

Then he picked up his phone, "Arkadiy, would you come here?"

Guessing that Grigoriy would talk about the file, Arkadiy came with the file. When he saw that Galina was there, he held the file parallel to his leg, making it impossible to read the title of the file.

"Arkadiy, Miss Galina is going to work with us. I want you to briefly explain the stage of the case and I want to learn Miss Galina's opinion."

Arkadiy said while he was looking at her smilingly,

"Our French source in the USA notified that he was being followed. Our source wants us to get him to our country. He is a superior officer. We can't risk it. Therefore, there is no time to investigate who has been following him or why before sending a team to counter-follow. We are discussing how we can get our source here with the lowest risk as soon as possible."

"Does he have a family?"

"No. He's single."

"Obviously, there is not a refugee situation."

"Absolutely."

"Then the solution is to get rid of the follower through disguise or to elude the follower. The last shot is to eliminate the followers. I think that when the sensitive relations with the USA considered, crashing into the follower car while they are following him with a car is the most sensible."

"We are evaluating all."

"What is on the routine walking route, can I look at that?"

Arkadiy passed the file, looking at Grigoriy.

Galina went through the file, squinting her eyes. After a couple minutes, "While our source is walking to the bus stop after he has left home, at this point (as she pointed) where the school bus stops to collect students, a second person wearing the same outfit with our source can get out of the bus, but he will need to introduce himself as a study teacher before he gets on the bus a couple of bus stops prior. If our source can get onto the bus while the second person leaves the bus, the second person will be able to change his clothes in a kind of way. He goes to the work, then he leaves the work in a short span of time and walks to the subway where he will be able to turn inside out his double-faced jacket. And he will be able to fold his trouser cuffs to his knees until it looks like shorts. And he has to pick the socks and the shoes in accordance with the shorts." Galina explained.

"Our source is a superior officer in an unofficial software company that belongs to the government. For this reason, he is wearing a suit all the time. It is rather hard for him to leave the workplace when he is in. He may draw attention. The crash idea is more sensible or that he can go to the indoor parking after he has left his cell phone at home, he can ask one of his neighbors to drive him to the main road where we will be able to pick him up is much more sensible." He explained.

"Then he must pick a car with a window film, right?" Galina asked.

"Or the method in which we can go with a removal van and pick him up is among the possibilities," Arkadiy answered.

"Thank you for your contribution, Miss Galina. Now you can go inside and meet your fellow co-workers." Grigoriy said.

When Galina left the room, she thought to herself, "I hope I performed well."

The acquaintance phase passed quickly. Everybody looked so tired and anxious. It was obvious that everybody was working until late hours.

Galina spent her first day by examining a couple of files that had been assigned to her. After preparing solution proposals, she took them to Grigoriy. But before she went in, she called him and asked his permission to which he answered, "Of course, come in."

When Galina entered the room, Grigoriy and Arkadiy were drinking whiskey. Both looked quite joyous.

"It is a pleasure to see you happy. I believe that the operation was a success." Galina said.

"The operation had already been over while we were asking about your opinion. But since we thought he would give away the name of the country to which he sold the information in cases where he was captured, we executed before he even left his home. And we completely solved the case." Grigoriy said.

Galina smiled, saying, "That was what I was expecting from you." The lives of people did not matter. The most important thing is to work without mistakes and not to take risks.

*

Galina was quite tired because of her heavy job workload, trainings, and meetings with Doruk in third countries. The fact that Doruk was kept under pressure was saddening and bothering Galina. Galina could not get pregnant despite all efforts. She thought that the reason might be stress.

Galina and Grigoriy were getting along well. She was meeting with Grigoriy's mother who he had found years later. She was also meeting with his father who had treated him horribly and put him off. Many of Russians might not meet with those who abandoned them, in this case, his father and mother. In short, they might exclude them from their lives.

Grigoriy had never mentioned his father and mother to Galina. It was not wise to expect him to mention them at their workplace.

While she was going into Grigoriy's rooms, she would confine herself to unbutton her blouse and show her suspenders by crossing her legs when she wore a miniskirt. Galina knew from his glances that he was charmed by her. But they had to stay separated in the workplace.

The days were passing quickly. It was one week before Galina's birthday. Galina kept in mind that Grigoriy was quite neat and was putting everything symmetrically in his room.

Galina was constantly changing her plans to reach Grigoriy in the way she wanted on her birthday. What if she took champagne and cake to Grigoriy who was a symmetry and order patient and ensured that he got angry, and kissed him to apologize? Then she said to herself "Come off it!"

The most reasonable solution was to state Grigoriy that she wanted to sleep with him. If Gregory had found out that he had been lured in, he would have withdrawn himself because of his professional reflexes, taken Galina into inter-rogation, and unwanted things might happen afterward.

This was why she had to act clearly.

She had a couple of deficiencies for preparation. She finalized her plan at the end of her shift. Before she headed home, she went to an optician and to a cosmetician. After wandering around for a while, she took the things she wanted and got out. Upon arriving home, she worked on her make-up and her hair. Her eyes were red. But she was prepared for it.

When she went to the workplace the next day, there was a rush once again. She did not know whether Grigoriy was in his office or not. He would make important meetings in the afternoon.

When she was back from lunch, she asked her co-worker Inga, "Is Mr. Grigory in a good mood, today?" Galina asked.

"He seemed quite happy. But if you want to take time off from work, you need to tell him a couple days before. He is not open to taking offs for the next day."

"I was going to submit a report. I just didn't want to come up to his anger moments."

Before her shift ended, she texted to Grigoriy, "I am grateful for that you supported my idea instead of Arkadiy's in the last meeting. It is my birthday tomorrow. I always make myself a wet-cake the day before my birthday. If you would be kind enough to give your address to me, I'll come by and give you some."

When Grigoriy read the message, "Another bitch that wants to take Arkadiy's place." He said to himself. He typed, "Odesskaya ulitsa, 22/6 Zyuzino, 2200" as an answer.

When Galina read the message, "Zyuzino, classy-boy-hood" she whimpered and texted "See you later."

Galina quickly went home. "Can you prepare some quick snacks for me? I'll go to the opera." She said. "With whom?" Darya asked. "Who would it be? With Olga, of course." She said and continued, "Maybe I'll stay at her place."

*

Galina was quite excited when she left home. Her plan was ready. She bought a sour-cherry Roshen cake from the market down the street. She had already called and requested a cab before she left home. The moment she got into the taxi, "I'll go somewhere that sells European liqueur and then to Zyuzino." She said. "Alright."

The cab driver replied. After driving for approximately 15 minutes, he pulled off the road, saying, "There." He pointed at a market, "It's open till 1:00 am."

"It's a little bit far, but still good." She replied.

Galina went into the market and bought Moet Champagne and Rafael Chocolates. Then she got into the cab, again. She had Doruk on her mind. "Doruk... If you weren't in this corrupted system, I would find a way to get out, even if I had to change sides." She thought to herself. Since the taxi driver entered the exact address to his smartphone, he pulled off the road at the number 22.

Galina paid for the cab service and got out of the car, saying, "Thank you."

The building security asked her which number she came to.

"Six."

"Your name?"

"Galina."

The officer picked up the phone, "You have a visitor named Galina, alright..." Then he hung up the phone. He accompanied Galina till the elevator after he pointed the way with his hand as if saying "go ahead." Galina got on the elevator. The security officer pressed the button of the third floor and smiled.

Galina took a deep breath. When she came to the floor, she looked at himself again in the mirror. Yes, she looked like Valeriya.

She rang the doorbell. Grigoriy opened the door. Grigoriy's smiling face suddenly changed to a serious expression. "New age, new appearance, I guess," Grigoriy said.

"Back to my original form, we could say. I've always felt myself like this." Galina answered.

Galina's attitude was also serious. She stepped inside with confidence. She turned her back to Grigoriy so that he would take her fur-coat off from her shoulders. Grigoriy took the fur-coat, opened the sliding wardrobe, and hung the fur-coat inside. But since he was a little bit confused, he said, "Come to the table." without sliding it back.

Galina sat at the table. She started to open the bag that she was holding and said, "I was not able to make a cake since my appearance change took a little while, but I bought a cake and champagne." Grigoriy was still glancing at Galina confusedly. Galina stood up and went to the kitchen, saying "I'll get glasses and a knife from the kitchen." She took two champagne glasses. "Let me bring the service pieces," Grigoriy said. He brought plates and cutlery.

He put them on the table. He was keeping his serious and dull stance. Galiba took the knives and forks. She put them on the table, next to the plates. Grigoriy opened the champagne bottle so carefully so that it would not pop. Not a drop of the alcohol should go for nothing.

"I always look at myself from outside. While happy and sad. "Somehow, I see myself like this. I have never tried forelocks and blue lenses. I really loved this appearance of mine. What do you think, Grigoriy? Galina asked.

"Since you address to me with my name even before getting drunk, there's no harm in telling you that you look rather beautiful."

Galina smiled. Grigoriy filled the glasses and said, "Let's make a toast to your new appearance." Galina smiled and drank a few sips.

After chatting for close to three hours, Galina and Grigoriy had already downed three bottles of champagne and one bottle of wine. When they were close to finishing the last bottle, Galina stood up from her chair and sat down next to Grigoriy.

Galina looked at Grigoriy straight in the eye for a long time and hugged him. Even though he was expecting to be kissed, he responded by hugging her. Galina held and placed Grigoriy's face on her shoulder. Grigoriy left his head on Galina's shoulder with the pleasantness of alcohol.

Galina seemed to be acting quite freely, but she was not giving up on controlling herself.

Grigoriy lifted his head and looked at Galina and said, "I have to confess something to you." Galina looked at his eyes and slightly squinted her eyes as if approving.

"You look very much like Valeriya."

"Your ex-wife?"

"No, my mother."

Galina placed Grigoriy's head on her shoulder one more time. Then she started to stroke his hair. Grigoriy began to pass out. She held Grigoriy's hand and took him to the sofa. Grigoriy was about to pass out. Galina sat next to him. She took his hand.

In the morning, Grigoriy got out of the sofa, wore his slippers, and realized that the knees of his trousers were wrinkled. "Guess I slept like crazy," he thought to himself and continued, "Galina must have gone to the bedroom." When he went into the bedroom, Galina woke up because of the sound and opened her eyes and looked at Grigoriy. She raised her hands and yawned while she covered her mouth with her hands.

"It was a delicate night, Grigoriy."

"The parts I remember were good, but I'm not responsible for the parts that I don't remember."

"Come next to me, we'll leave after laying down a bit."

Grigoriy took off his trousers and went to bed. Galina wrapped her arm around his head. And she started to stroke his hair with her other hand. Grigoriy was as if he was about to pass out.

"It is enough that I stroke your hair and give love. Now, I'll go home, remove my lenses, adjust my hair, and go to the headquarters." She said.

"Why don't you come like this?"

"It would bother you that people hit on someone who resembles your mother, would it?"

"It would."

Galina kissed Grigoriy on the cheek while she was leaving. "See you later." Grigoriy said. "Valeriya will not be coming in the evening, but Galina will come at the same time. If you have an appointment, cancel it." Galina replied. Grigoriy nodded.

When Galina came home, the mole mark on her face was still there. She looked quite characteristic. She went to the bathroom. She cleaned her makeup using a make-up wipe. The remains of chestnut brown hair dye were still on the edge of the sink. It was the first time that she had dyed her hair that fast. She removed her lenses. Then she put them in the solution. She was rather disturbed to sleep with lenses. Her eyes were red. "The task comes first." She said to herself. She sprinkled her forelock at first. Then she stuck her forelock together to the side with mousse. Her hair became a little bit wavy, then the writing on the bottle caught her attention. It was saying, "for wavy hair." "Subconscious is like that. Even the smallest fonts were engraved in my subconscious." She said to herself.

She changed her clothes and wore fancy ones. She wore a long, flowery dress just like in the photo, in which Grigoriy had been one-year-old and his father, mother, and himself were present and which had been taken in a photo studio, to resemble Valeriya. These clothes were fashionable in those years. However, Russian women preferred mini-skirts rather than long dresses now. Galina wore something suitable for her birthday. Blue would suit her. When she heard the door opened, "Gala, are you available?" Her mother asked.

"Yep."

"I wanted to celebrate your birthday first, but I guess you didn't see the text I sent you at midnight.

"Yes, I didn't see that one, mom."

They hugged each other. "I wish you health, happiness, and success, my daughter. I wish everything would go just the way you want. Your only goal should not be money nor career. Just focus on happiness." Darya made a wish.

"Thank you, mom."

"Go to the kitchen and wait for me," Darya said. Galina went into the kitchen. Darya came with a bouquet of flowers and a box with a bow wrapped around, saying, "Surprise!"

"Mommy, you always make me happy on every birthday of mine," Galina said. She hugged and kissed her mother. She untied the bow wrapped around the box. She opened her present package with care so that it would not tear.

Her mother had magnified Galina's favorite childhood picture and had framed it. Galina's eyes were brimmed with tears. She returned to those years for a moment. A lot had changed since then.

Galina's father had passed away in a traffic accident while Galina had been in Turkey during the murder of John.

*

When Galina went to the office, everyone was smiling to her, her close friends hugged and kissed her, and those who were not her close friends shook her hand and wished her happy birthday. At the end of the day, they were talking about that everybody had been invited to the celebration in Mr. Grigoriy's office. "I guess they will never stop perceiving this job as a job," Arkadiy said to himself.

Everyone headed to the Grigoriy's room, holding their presents. Galina rose from her desk. She adjusted her dress. She happily entered Grigoriy's room. She blew the candles, cut the cake, received her presents; everyone was quite happy. Grigoriy's glances towards Galina was sincere and warm. Neither of them wanted to reveal anything around.

Galina left her workplace happily, holding the bags of her presents. While she was leaving, Inga said, "Let me drop you off."

"I would love to."

"The thing that I hate the most is that when I start drinking, I cannot drink enough," Inga said and Galina laughed out loud.

"Same here," Galina replied.

They kept on talking about women and men under the influence of alcohol while they were on their way. While Galina was getting out of the car, she said, "Thank you very much." and took the bags in the back after opening the door of the car.

When she got home, she showed the presents she had received to her mother. Darya looked at every one of the presents. She quite liked the white blouse with shiny flakes. "Who bought that?" Darya asked.

"Yuriy."

"Then who gave the Soviet Union and Tsarist Russia pictures?"

"Arkadiy. Even his presents are ideological."

"Arkadiy thinks that Russians should have a greater piece of land and be a superpower, just like the Turks.

"Today, we are going to a home of a female co-worker of mine and throw a children's party."

"I've heard pajama parties before, but I've never heard of a children's party, what is that?"

"We'll dress up like children and do makeup."

"This is the new fashion, I suppose."

Galina went into the bathroom without a response. She glanced at the mirror. She painted her cheeks close to pink. She parted her hair in the middle. "Mom, would you plait my hair?" She called to her mother.

Darya came to the bathroom and asked, "Two plaits at sides?" Darya plaited her hair that was parted in the middle. Galina really looked like a child.

Galina picked the yellow lipstick and the lip liner from the cosmetics that she had bought recently. She shortened her fuchsia skirt. She pulled her sports socks until her knees. She wore the expensive white blouse that Yuriy got for her to hit on her. She rolled up her sleeves. She needed to add some sexiness. She took off her white sports socks and wore her skin color suspenders. Then she put on her white sports socks. Now she was ready. As a part of her plan, she did not forget the balloon with Tweety on it that she had bought from a mall. The balloon did not pop, but it was not flying anymore.

"Should I buy alcohol again?" As she was thinking that, the bottles in the showcase of Grigoriy crossed her mind. Every one of them was expensive than the other.

She called a cab. When she got out of the building, she felt so cold. "Of course, the effect of alcohol began to wear off now." She thought to herself.

He went into the back seat of the car and told the driver the address. She got out of the cab. She looked at herself in the plate glass as a whole. "Delicately beautiful, just like what I wanted." She said to herself.

When she entered the building, the security officer asked for her name and the number of the apartment she came to. When Galina came to the door, she noticed that she was quite excited and an hour early. She rang the doorbell. Grigoriy opened the door, and said, "Welcome, little Galina."

Galina went in. She turned to Grigoriy and said, "Do you know what I despise the most, Grisha?" Grigoriy shook his head and pursed like a child.

"Not enough drinking, when starting drinking." She said. There was nothing like taking the useful things for her. "Thank you, Inga." She said to herself. "I was drinking, but when the door was knocked, I panicked thinking that the teacher had come." Grigoriy childishly said.

Galina was jumping around and acting as if she was a child in the house; she was running around the table and stick her hands into Grigoriy's ears to make funny noises. Grigoriy was also acting and making jokes as if he was a child. The drinks they had been consuming caused them to be drunk. Galina took Grigoriy's hand and took him to the bedroom.

She sat on Grigoriy's lap. Then she started kissing him slowly. Grigoriy was kissing Galina and taking off his trousers, on the other hand.

After long lasting sex, Grigoriy decided to ejaculate himself with his hand. Because the strong medications were preventing him from ejaculating.

Galina was watching Grigoriy and doing things with her tongue which could be perceived both sexy and childish. Grigoriy finally began cramping as he reached climax. When Grigoriy climaxed, Galina applauded and laughed like a child, saying, "You did it!" Grigoriy's happiness and tiredness could be understood from his face.

"Where is the blouse that stupid Yuriy had bought?" she thought to herself as she was looking around. She thought for a moment to clean up the sperm with that blouse. "But how could I go home, then?" She said to herself.

Looking at Galina, Grigoriy thought to himself, "There's no one happier than you, deception master; love, sex, and a lovely togetherness."

*

Galina kept reading the file quickly. The appointment order would be given tomorrow, and she had to meet with Grigoriy. It had been mentioned that he had the brightest future and he had been filling his pockets the most during his tasks. Grigoriy had the two elements combined. Money and success. Which one was important for him more than SVR? Success? Or money? It did not matter much. Success always brought money along.

Galina told Doruk, "I've identified the basic patterns now." Convey them now so that they return quickly to tell me what it would be best to do. His first girlfriend was at an age a little bit greater than his peers. He could be considered as an adult when he had his first girlfriend. His marriage lasted quite short. I reviewed all the photos in the file. I was able to look like his mother with some makeup. Could I be his "psychological mother" maybe? Motherly love is the only thing that he sought and couldn't find. Convey them all. Do you hear me, Doruk?"

Galina woke up, wandering, "Doruk... Doruk..." She said to herself, "It's seriously dangerous that I have dreamed about a meeting with Doruk." She straightened up on the bed, turned on the sleeping berth lamp, put the quilt aside, and wore her slippers. She went to the bathroom and washed her face. Then she went to the kitchen and had a glass of water. She got back to her bed and continued to sleep.

Doruk had also complicated dreams that night. He dreamed of the place where his father had died as a martyr. At the same time, a moment of the funeral cross swam before his eyes. He saw huge Turkish flags and pictures of Atatürk. For a moment, he was riding a horse. Then his gaze suddenly turned to Galina. Then to Atatürk. Atatürk was delivering a speech from the dais of the Assembly.

He sharply woke up. "Let it be good!" He thought to himself. Just like Galina, Doruk drank a glass of water and continued to sleep.

"Son, did you wake up in the night?" His mother asked when it was morning.

"Yes, I had complicated dreams."

"Then, don't tell me, son. "You seem to be nervous, is there a problem?"

"Actually, no, but I don't know."

"Whatever comes, it comes from Allah. Don't forget that, my son. "Always be careful while you work, don't cheat somebody of their rights, don't break hearts."

"Mom, you know that my job issues a deception license."

"The government may use tricks in its works, don't worry; it uses all the methods that you've been working on."

Doruk was affected by his dream when he had seen the funeral, the flags, and Galina and when he had heard the voice of Atatürk.

It was Saturday. He called his manager and asked, "Hello, Sir. Are you available?" His manager replied, "I believe so." "Would you mind if I came in the afternoon?" He asked. His manager said, "Alright." and hung up the phone.

He left his house, got into his car, and he went to Lake Eymir. He parked his car in the parking area. "It's good to take a short walk." He said to himself. He was used to having a pair of comfortable shoes in his car for his field work.

He took the shoes out of the trunk. He sat down in the front seat and changed his shoes. Then started walking. He came to a buffet at the edge of the lake. It was crowded as always. All of the people were standing up, and the back wheels of the bicycles were attached to a giant parking iron. The bicycles were colorful. He headed for the buffet.

When it was his turn, he asked, "Can I get an eggplant flapjack and a glass of tea?" The cashier lady yelled, "Eggplant three!" and told him that he could take the tea from the side of the buffet. After receiving the change, he filled his own the at the side. After waiting for a few minutes while standing, the flapjack lady asked, "Waiting for potato?" It seemed that she meant potato flapjack. "No, I was waiting for the eggplant flapjack." He answered. The lady said, "Just a minute." Then she passed the tray.

Doruk sat on the stool. And he put the tray on his knees. He started to eat his flapjack with joy. He was also sipping his tea between bites. The temperature of the tea intensified the steam coming out of his mouth. Doruk started to listen to the two men who came and sat by his side.

"My friend... "Look at our ancestors, then look at us. Look what life has turned us into."

"Life has been what it used to be. There were also people who practiced usury, gambled, and allowed gambling. They were all there."

"Let me ask you a question, see if you can answer it. My father's grandfather who passed away was a true Muslim. His name was İsmail. He was so diligent that my aunts could get enough water for him from the water spout in the village. He was consistently taking a shower. Huh, don't forget that there were no cars, no money. He made the pilgrimage by walking and sometimes by carriage. He returned a few months later. In short, Grandpa İsmail was rather a good Muslim. And the question is, "Grandpa İsmail would not eat eggs in summer, why?"

"Eggs stink during the summer?"

"No."

"Is it a detail about the fertilization and egg production of chickens?"

"No, it's a completely religious detail. You're lazy, if you come to walk with me the next week at the same time, I'll give you the answer. But think about that during the week. Inquire about its answer."

Doruk started to think the answer to the question. Then he returned to his car and headed for his workplace.

When he came home in the evening, he made so much egg-related research on his computer. But he failed to find a completely religious answer. "Saturday, 10:00-Eymir" he noted on his phone and begun looking forward to the next week to learn the answer to the question.

*

Galina accomplished many tasks thanks to the supports of Grigoriy and Doruk who represented the National Intelligence Service. Her qualities such as her different and creative approach to events, providing multiple solution proposals at a time, reviewing every possibility created the thought on her co-workers' mind that she was a labyrinth.

The relationship between Galina and Grigoriy was no secret, anymore.

The weeks passed as they discussed the wedding date.

"How romantic, G&G. I wish the wedding date was a day which is also the month, and which is a lucky day according to the Chinese calendar." Inna told.

"If I know Mister Grigoriy, he would never marry someone," Yuriy answered.

With all his seriousness, Arkadiy told, "Guys, stop talking about Galina and Grigoriy and their wedding date. Let's mind our own business."

Inga whimpered to herself, "Tempers flared as the floor got slippery."

Galina's goal was not to take Arkadiy's position anymore, Grigoriy was already his manager. His main goal was to make Grigoiry a Director with the information to be provided by Turks and through successful operations.

Grigoriy was extremely open to Galina. But when it was about business, he was preserving his stance in which he valued the rules of the profession the most. When Galina would come into his room, he would turn the documents back or tell Galina, "Would you come a few minutes later," or "I'll call you when I'm done."

Galina was not getting what she wanted from Grigoriy. It was obvious he needed more time. When she would start getting information, she was going to plan a marriage to establish a healthy information flow and to keep it long-lasting. Since she did not get what she wanted, she had to postpone the wedding.

One day after work, Inga asked, "As far as I know, you're seeing a source from abroad, are you sleeping with him?" Galina's response was interesting, "Depends on the content of the information he brings."

"So, has Grigoriy talked to you on this subject?" "No."

"So, he has never asked you whether you were sleeping with him or not?"

"Sex? Who cares? The important thing is the task and you know that; if we don't do our jobs well, our whole society will polish others' knob."

"You are right."

"Have you ever slept with one of your sources?"

"Let me think. I would actually provide a clearer answer if you asked whether I had one source that I haven't slept with."

"You get your sources in free and with laughter and profit on the treasury."

"Joke aside, I turned the most of them into sources with money. And to celebrate my successes, I slept with whoever I desired. So, have you accomplished tasks using the sex card?"

"Yes..."

"Then you are following the method that was taught to us well, 'Wet the thread so well that it would easily get through the hole of the needle; otherwise, no matter how thin the thread is, it won't get through.'"

"I try to do everything the best I can do."

"Then, let me ask you a question, I earned this, right?"

"Yep."

"How do you know a man?"

"You go first, then me..."

"From the darkness between his pupil and the sclera. What about you?"

"I know a man in bed."

Such an answer would be expected from Galina. They burst into laughter.

*

Doruk invited Galina to France. Galina went outside before she met Doruk. While she was wandering around, she was looking at showcases. She also checked whether she was being followed or not by casually shopping in the stores.

"I'll go to the big store ahead, lastly." She thought. Before arriving Paris, she was about to complete the test which she had been doing on the follower determination route.

She went to her hotel and started waiting for Doruk.

When Doruk came to her room, they called a cab and went out. They walked for a while. The time had passed so fast that it was getting dark as they talked. Doruk started to tell Galina about a rocket system that had been tried to mount onto a car whose brand and model he did not know. He gave a lot of detailed information about the rocket system. Galina began to speak and asked, "Is there anything else?"

Doruk dogmatized, "No." Galina turned off the audio and video recorder.

*

Doruk came home after work. It was quite a tiring day. "My son, you have been staying at home on weekends, lately?" Her mother commented. Doruk dropped the subject, saying, "Just a coincidence, mom."

Since Elif thought that Doruk was in low spirits, she looked for a subject and told the first one that had crossed her mind, "I shared the subject that you told me, about not eating eggs in summer, with your aunts. No one could figure out the answer. I told them that since chickens do not stay in the coop in summer and go into the gardens of neighbors to find food, and they feed on things

96

without gaining their consent, which will make it haram. Then I told them that the eggs to be gathered will also be haram since the food was consumed without the land owner's approval and gave the example, "The fruit of the poisonous tree will also be poisonous."

"Nice one, mom," Doruk said and fell asleep on the couch.

*

There was a change in plans since Grigoriy was still not at a point that had been desired.

"When the music changes, so does the dance."

African Proverb

Galina was going to take the position of Arkadiy. In this way, Grigoriy would have to carry out the operations with Galina, not Arkadiy.

"After Arkadiy's dismissal, how good it would be if he chose someone who had been his co-worker for a long time as his assistant. If the plan makers in Turkey decided that it would be the best, it would be the best. The Turks probably learned how to ski by slipping that much, they have not recovered since Hürrem in the Ottoman Palace." She said.

She pictured Arkadiy before her eyes. Just like Grigoriy, Arkadiy had been successful at his job and meddled with businesses that involved so much money including financial institutions and because of this, he had put on weight.

She had heard that Inga and Arkadiy had slept a couple times. She couldn't ask Inga about Arkadiy's address, nor could she ask Grigoriy. So, how would she find his address? Should she meet with the Personnel Manager, again? The Turks had told Galina through Doruk that Arkadiy's family might be living out of town, that they might have sent a package to him, and this was why she might his address by asking the company about his address, giving his name and surname. But when Arkadiy's name was searched by any branch of the cargo company, a notice may be sent to the headquarters. This was why it was very dangerous. Following Arkadiy was a less harmful method.

Arkadiy's daughter would come to his house from time to time. He was also separated from his wife, too. For a moment, she thought whether it would produce a result if she had blackmailed Arkadiy through his daughter. Arkadiy was a man of faith. Faithful people would generally submit to the blackmail and report the situation instead of betraying. For this reason, it was not an option.

Galina thought that it would be useful to talk to Inga first. She thought that she would invite Inga to a nice pub on Saturday night. Since Inga loved wandering around and having fun, she would accept her offer and she did.

Inga became so drunk that she even told Galina that she had divorced her husband after finding out that her husband had cheated on her with his brother on new year's eve. Galina told her, "I have never thought that you would be such a whore." and they laughed.

Inga wanted to go to a nightclub. They got into Inga's car. Inga was able to drive her car even though she was drunk.

Since there were no free tables in the nightclub, Inga immediately wanted to sit at the table where three men were sitting. The men accepted their offer and instantly made room for them. Galina started to smoke the hookah that Inga ordered while they were sipping their whiskey. Galina was smoking the hookah with the same mouthpiece as a sign of sincerity.

Galina was trying to respond to the toast that was raised by the men while she was trying to eat her toast that they had ordered and to bring up the subject about Arkadiy:

"Why didn't you marry to Arkadiy?"

"Arkadiy is a psycho. He is not for me, all he thinks is his job. He starts working even in the Sunday morning."

"What about his daughter? Doesn't he take care of her?"

"He pretends to do so. He thinks that he is fathering well by checking who she hangs up with and her phone, which shows that he follows her."

"Arkadiy would pull himself together if you established a good relationship with his daughter, right?"

"Impossible."

"You would have tried at least by taking his daughter for a couple weekends."

"I don't care anymore."

When Galina realized that Inga dropped the subject, she did not want to proceed further within the subject. Inga was also a member of the service. She might report the indirect questions that focused on Arkadiy.

Galina tried to come up with a solution the next day. Then she comforted herself by saying, "Let Turks find it." She was going to send an encrypted message to Doruk. If she was unable to obtain Arkadiy's address, she was going to put a crying smile at the end of the text. Therefore, finding his address would be the task of the National Intelligence Service.

A few days later, she texted to Doruk, telling him that she had missed him with a crying smile at the end of the text.

*

The only thing that Galina had to do was to learn the name of the spies standing by in the USA. But this one was the most difficult.

At the beginning of each month, there were routine meetings about the situation in the USA.

Galina was not allowed to attend these meetings. It could be quite risky for her to request that. Grigoriy was seeing her as his mother and his little girlfriend, but she did not even want to think about the possibility in which things would go off the rail. Grigoriy was very cruel. He could wipe everything away, put her in jail, torture her, and eventually execute her.

Galina was going to ask for help from Turkey, from Doruk about this matter. They arranged a routine lover's meeting, again. This time, the meeting was in Uzbekistan. Doruk had put on almost two kilograms in days since he had eaten so much Uzbek pilaf.

Galina told Doruk about her plan. Doruk leaned the brand of the overhead projector that was in the meeting room. He was going to request a device to be mounted on the overhead, which would allow them to record the information reflected.

"Galina, if we find such a device, they will send it to you somehow. Know that if I send you a picture of us, the device has been found."

"Okay, I'll wait for it. I don't like the system and managers of ours. I want the system to change and conservatives to be gone, but I cannot put myself in jeopardy anymore. Please let them know about these. Be a little upright, they are not going to put you in jail anymore. I became one of their best guys, relax. You know that I cannot get pregnant under pressure, right?"

"I talked to the clinic on the phone. First, they suggested that we should take a stress-free vacation about 15-20 somewhere hot. They also advised that we should use pollen whose brand I cannot recall and try again."

It was true that Doruk had called the clinic, but they had informed him that he was infertile, and he needed a long-term therapy.

*

Galina was startled by Grigoriy who suddenly got out of the bed since he was being called to the headquarters to direct an operation!

"Where are you, Grigoriy?"

"They called from the headquarters, I guess there's something important."

"Do you want me to make coffee?"

"Thanks. I'll drink when I reach there."

Galina realized that Grigoriy had still not come when she woke up in the morning. When she looked at her phone, she saw the pictures that Doruk had sent with a text saying, "To you." Galina understood that the device had been found and felt relieved.

Galina started to wander around on Sunday so that they would communicate to her. She ran the application which counted her steps on her phone. Then started walking. She was not checking whether she was being followed or not. Because the Turks were likely to follow her so that they would give her the device at an appropriate place.

After walking for about 45 minutes, she stopped to buy a coffee from the buffet on the sidewalk. After she drank her coffee, she continued walking. She started to look at some showcases and stores. Then she decided to return home. She went to the grocery store near her house. She bought some cleaning materials. She paid for them at the checkout. The cashier smilingly said, "See you later," Galina was expecting a communication of any means. But it did not happen. She came home. She ate her lunch. She took a shower, then she decided to lay down for a bit.

It was beneficial for her to meet her co-workers outside of their workplace to increase their sincerity. But she gave up on calling Inga at the last minute and called Olga:

"Ola, hello. Want to meet with me at GUM? What do you say, I've missed you so much."?

"Me too. We'll meet at the entrance at 6:00 pm, deal?"

"Deal."

They met in front of the mall. They went to the restaurant that Galina recommended for dinner. The reason why Galina wanted to eat at this restaurant was that the restroom was genderless. She thought that maybe the person who would deliver the device would do so easily in the restroom.

She went into the bathroom. After she left the cabin, there was no one to approach her while she was washing her hands. "I suppose they have failed to bring the device." She whimpered.

They left the mall. Galina told Olga, "Maybe, I'll pay a visit to Grigoriy. I'll take a cab." She kissed Olga and got into the cab that was waiting for her. She waited for a while before she went into her house, but no communication was established.

The next day was a day of routine for her. She was constantly thinking, "Maybe they have been waiting, thinking that I would be under custody since I have been getting close with Grigoriy.

After leaving the workplace, she headed for home, yawning on the way. Thinking must have tired her. Grigoriy had not been seen around until the evening.

An elderly woman sat next to her before she left the bus. She had a small purse in her hand. Just as Galina was about to get off the bus, the lady passed a pair of earbuds folded roundly and pointed somewhere as if she was asking directions for a place and explained, "I'll receive it in the same way. It starts working when mounted and records only video for 12 hours."

"Yes, I suppose the old building on this street had been demolished and this one was built instead of that," Galina replied. She put the earbuds in her pocket as she talked. She got off the bus and headed for her home. She was very curious about the device. If she had her druthers, she would run to home and check it as soon as possible, but it would also draw attention.

When she came home, her mother welcomed Galina with a warm smile as usual. They had dinner and chatted. Galina told her that she had been tired and wanted to sleep early. She took the device out. Then she unfolded the earbuds.

There was a thin lens in white plastic. Since this lens would be mounted exactly on the lens of the projection device and in the shape of a cone that grew in parallel with the projection lens, recognizing it was out of the subject.

She immediately called Grigoriy,

"Where have you been today, tell me."

"Unexpected things, you know."

"I miss you, I'll come to your place soon."

"Okay."

Galina could only enter the room with the device alongside Grigoriy. Otherwise, she had to enter the headquarters through highly-sensitive detection devices. Of course, she had to leave the headquarters alongside Grigoriy.

*

When Galina delivered the device to the elderly lady, she got out of the bus and took a deep breath. She had planted the devices, received, and delivered it back without any obstructions. But she would always think pessimistically in important tasks as if something bad was going to happen. When she completed her task, she thought, "I knew that would end up well."

*

When Galina uttered statements that gave no any other option to Grigory while keeping her serious stance, Grigoriy would do what he had been told as if he was under hypnosis. Grigoriy had surrendered to Galina's maternal domination. But when it came to SVR, Grigoriy suddenly came to his senses and came out of Galina's dominance.

"Motherly love cannot be created."

Erich Fromm

The fact that Grigoriy could not be utilized as desired was because of his unconditional patriotism and his disciplined training in the Soviet Union period. Even though people would reveal their secrets to their mother and father, Grigoriy was not telling anything or revealing any secrets about his job to Galina who he loved as if she had been her mother, except for his private life, friendships, traumatic events he had experienced in the military school. This condition was bothering the Turks.

Galina was tired and bored of playing with a big baby.

Grigoriy and Arkadiy had been working together in complete harmony for a long time. After meetings that took hours, the National Intelligence Service decided to target Arkadiy for the elimination of Grigoriy, the replacement of Grigoriy with Arkadiy or for the dissolution of the entire Department of America. Causing a member of the rival service who had been doing his job excellently to dysfunction would be a great success, after all. The main goal here was to set five members who had the veto power in the UN against themselves, which would lead to a change in the structure.

Doruk stated his concern by saying that Galina would be taken into interrogation and she would give herself away or maybe even not be able to pass the lie test in cases in which Arkadiy was treated as a traitor. In this context, Doruk's manager said, "These are always possible, Galina was one of the rare women, who was allowed to the AVR (Foreign Intelligence Academy, SVR's school). She'll get through all these. I have no doubt about that. You can trust your source and relax. Even though we haven't discussed it thoroughly, Galina will be protected if SVR pursues the wrong person."

*

Arkadiy's address was eventually found after a sensitive following operation. Galina was very nervous while she was waiting for the results. Now, it was the second phase of the plan.

Discoveries around Arkadiy's house in many different disguises had been made. Arkadiy's routine behaviors and acts had been observed for a month. Four different teams had been assigned to these observations.

Finally, everything that was to be done was planned. The planning was completed after a 12-hour study in Turkey.

Arkadiy was calling the shop under his house to order a beer, a few days a week. Kristina with whom Galina worked with in the church got out of his car whose brand was Mercedes and shopped for a while. When she saw the delivery guy who was taking the beers upstairs, she lifted her arm and said,

"Hey, young man!"

"Yes?"

"Can you help me to the car?"

"Alright."

After they left the store, while they were placing the bags in the trunk of the car, the young man was looking at the car's exhaust.

"How fast can you drive with this car?"

"240 km/hour."

"Cool."

"Can I ask for your help?"

"Sure." "I will bring your orders wherever you live."

"Not orders. I'll ask for help from you for a little bit different subject and I'll provide you with a little financial support."

"I'll do whatever you want." (Still looking at the car.)

"What's your name?"

"Anton."

"Okay Anton, I'm the wife of the guy who drinks a lot and lives in the third floor of the opposite building. We've been living apart for a while. I want you to check whether there's another woman in his house, would you do it?"

"Will I enter the house with a key?" (In panic)

"No, you are going to give him this bag. There's another bag in it. You'll deliver his order with this little bag in it as if you forgot it inside. There's a cigarette inside it. You'll give this. Of course, you'll put his drinks in the bag. It's the same as yours. After he has closed the door, you'll deliver another order to an apartment near. If there are no orders, you'll go to a lower floor and then go up once again. You'll press the doorbell again and say to him, 'There was another order in the bag, cigarettes, I wrapped it in a bag, can I get it back?' Let's see if my husband or his girlfriend opens the door when you ring the doorbell the second time. And tell me the results. I'll stop by around noon. But you are going to give that bag back to me, understood? And I will give you an amount of money that is enough for the latest Playstation that you want. But you won't tell anyone about me, okay?"

"Okay, it's easy."

"Antonichka, if you don't want to witness the divorce, if you are afraid of my husband, only touch the handles of the bag, do not touch the bag itself. Okay, you understand? Otherwise, "the judge will summon you too.""

"Okay."

"Then you'll give me the bags back, but please be sure that you don't touch the bag or show it to anyone, alright?"

Anton nodded. Kristina took the bag out of her car. While she was handing it over to Anton, she pointed the handles of the bag and said, "Only touch these parts."

Kristina approached the shop in her car, four days later. He couldn't see Anton. She bought a few packs of cigarettes, then she left the store. While she was at the entrance, she saw that Anton was approaching.

"Anton, did you see the woman?"

"No, he opened the door again."

"Did you get the bag back?"

"Yep."

"Where is the bag now?"

"I hid it in the fuse box so that my boss wouldn't see it."

"See this piggy bank? The money inside this will be enough for anything that you want, come on now, get the bag back without touching it other than the handles."

Anton ran back to the back of the building. And he came with the bags in the same way he had gone. Anton was quite happy. Kristina instructed him, "You'll say 'I saved the money with tips' if someone asks about it. Did my husband checked whether there was a pack of cigarettes in the bag and look at you strangely?" She asked. Anton answered, "Yes, he unfolded the bag, checked inside, and gave it back to me."

An alcoholic man who had gradually started to visit the shop frequently and who was leaving without the change had improved his dialog with Anton's boss to gather information while Arkadiy had been investigated. The following dialogue had arisen after improving their sincerity.

"I was in prison in Arabia for a long time."

"That's tough."

"Do you know what I miss the most?"

"What?"

"Vodka"

"I love it too."

"Time has changed everything, even the taste of vodka."

"Everything is money now."

"Unfortunately." "I encountered Mister Arkadiy at the door the other and he pretended not to know me."

"Seriously?"

"Yeah, I won't look at his face again."

"Maybe he was down in the dumps?"

"Why would he be? Doesn't he have money?"

"I don't think he's short on money, considering that most orders have been his."

"I don't care even if he has a problem with money. Let him rot in hell, that pretending bastard."

When he came to the store, he would also observe Anton. One time, he was watching the TV in the store. His boss had turned the volume of the TV up. He said, "Look, Anton, it's the car show that you like."

"I drove this car at the Playstation Cafe," Anton replied.

There were also patterns of children!

*

First intervention to the diplomat who lost himself after he had been poisoned was performed where there were no cameras. Even though the Russian woman who performed the intervention told that she was alone, the man next to her scrabbled his pockets. The first thing that happened to those who died in Russia was the scrabbling. A water-proof and non-combustible bag of embassies had been left In the internal pocket of the diplomat, by a man who looked like a dilly-dallier, using a silicon solution that removed prints. There was an encrypted roll of paper and many numbers on it in the bag. It was a list and it contained the names of some of the standing by agents in the USA.

The handle of the bag had been cut. The nylon file material specially manufactured in the US was shaped into a bag by the members of the Turkish National Intelligence Service.

The FSB and SVR teams had reached the scene faster than Americans and searched the diplomat. The bad that had been found on the diplomat was taken and teams were gone in a short span of time. Other than the bag, the now-dead diplomat had some money and an identity card provided by Russian authorities indicating that he was a diplomat in his other pocket.

After a short time, KR Department officials raided American Department and took Arkadiy by pointing a gun against his head. Arkadiy was so confused that he couldn't say anything. Everyone was in shock. No explanation was made to Grigoriy. The glance of the head of the KR Department at Grigoriy was disturbing.

*

A day before the interrogation of Arkadiy, he came into Grigoriy's room and handed over a paper he was holding while Galina was also in the room. It was written on the paper that Grigoriy's friend in the Greek Service requested an immediate meeting. "Prepare and go to Greece as soon as possible." Grigoriy told Galina.

Galina wended her way with a small suitcase and an in-date fake passport which was authorized to provide entrance to Schengen countries in Europe and had entrance and exit stamps in order to leave an impression as if she was going there for a four-day vacation.

She was getting bored as she was waiting to board the plane. "Shouldn't I go to Greece, I wonder?" Galina thought. She needed to defuse her tension. She sat at the cafe right next to her, dragging her small suitcase. "You got dark beer?" Galina asked the waiter. "Unfortunately." The waiter responded. "Then, I'll take a glass of Chivas," Galina said. It was her first time drinking that early. It was the conclusion of the Greece task after all she had been through. "This is how you get into alcoholism." She said to herself.

She was smiling just like the other passengers on the plane when she boarded. She had not neglected to drink red wine with her dish. "It would be good if I slept until landing." She passed through. She was unable to sleep because of her anxiety, even though she was on the edge of falling asleep. Finally, they landed.

She left her anxiety behind as soon as she got out of the plane. She was walking upright and looking at the airport personnel right in the face and she was not turning her eyes away. When she came to the passport control point, she said to the policeman in English, smilingly, "Hello." "Why did you come to Athens?" The policeman asked. "Vacation," Galina answered, pretending that she did not know English. After receiving the seal, she entered the country. She did not like Athens International Airport that much. As she was leaving, she saw the stands of Turkish Tour companies and thought, "They are developing Greece to see Atatürk again, I suppose. That's the love for the leader!" she said to herself and had fun, making fun of it as she got into the service vehicle through the guidance of the tour companies at the airport exit. They also needed to board a ferry in order to go to Kea Island. "It's a so-called vacation, almost a cruelty," she thought.

Having settled in the hotel, her door was knocked a couple hours later. An old Greek person gave her a digital camera, saying "Dobre pajalivat tavarish, (Welcome comrade,)" and lurked out of sight after he turned back in the corridor. Galina thought his voice tone and his appearance were of a top-tier official. Galina went to the restaurant for lunch. While she was going to the restaurant, she saw that the old man was leaving the hotel, holding a small bag. It seemed like he had a quick vacation just like Galina!

She turned on the camera and wanted to look at the pictures as she was sitting at the restaurant. But it was completely forbidden to examine documents and their contents according to SVR rules. She hung it up on her shoulder from its strap. Then she listened to her inner voice and started looking at pictures.

In the first photo, a paper with writing, "Information was provided by well-sinkers. Photos of some National Intelligence Service members." could be seen. Galina did not know who these well-sinkers were.

The terror organization, named well-sinkers whose intention was to try to overthrow the elected government through a coup attempt in the following days, to kill people and dump them in wells. But fortunately, their intentions would be revealed soon. Since they received the well advice and the information on their whereabouts from foreign services, they were named as well-sinkers. The Turkish Government would give the name of "Fethullah Terrorist Organization (FETO) to this terror organization. Since Greece knew about their plan and decided to support them, the country was cooperating with the terror organization in question.

FETO also infiltrated the Turkish Intelligence Service. This terror organization was trying to cause National Intelligence Personnel to be demasked and to fail in their both domestic and foreign tasks, and to ensure that they would be executed within possibilities. They were sharing the information related to the personnel working in the field.

Galina figured out from the old man's method that he hadn't shared this information with an instruction from Greek National Intelligence Service (Ethniki Ypiresia Pliroforion, EYP). Because Greek authorities knew very well that Russia did not favor this organization. The old man's purpose was to ensure that Russians protected their countries. Saying "Comrade" to Galina was a sign of that.

Galina kept on looking at portraits and photographs taken in weddings of some Turkish National Intelligence Service members. In one of the photos, there were young people who formed a wolf gesture with their hands. She had learned about this gesture in her training and it was one of the greatest threat perceptions for Russia. "When you see this gesture, think about it as a triumph, as a victory." She was told in her training, but the foundation of the gesture had been built upon Turan ideology which aimed to gather all Turks in one country.

As she kept on examining photos, her inner voice told her to get back to the previous photo. The food she had ordered finally arrived. She put the camera on the table. She took a little piece of her food with a knife. She sipped her white wine.

When she got back to the photo, she saw young Doruk among the people who had performed the gesture. He was really Doruk. The names of the young people were written under the photo. At the rightmost side of the photograph, it was written "Teoman Gök." And Doruk was unmasked! Galina's eyes grew as if they were going to fall out of her skull. She felt faint with the shock she experienced. The first day on which they had met, their lovemaking, the moment in which Doruk told her that he had wanted a child, and the sentence she had read in a book in the bookstore in Baku flashed before her eyes, **"You'll be broken at where you broke."**

www.ingramcontent.com/pod-product-compliance
Lightning Source LLC
Chambersburg PA
CBHW071329130626
46556CB00004B/1814